Restlessness

Also by Lorne Shirinian

Poetry
Manuscript: Tom Sturgess
Armenian North American Poetry: An Anthology (edited and appeared in)
Poems of Dispersion and Other Rites of Movement
The Blue Heron Press Anthology (edited and appeared in)
Earthquake
Rough Landing
Rendering the Timeline (forthcoming)

Fiction
The Key and Other Stories
Beginnings and Ends
History of Armenia and Other Fiction
Memory's Orphans
When Darkness Falls Upon Us
Love Hemorrhage
What Remains
Transformations: Selected Short Fiction, 1977-2005

Drama
Exile in the Cradle
This Dark Thing: Two One-Act Plays
Monumental

Life Writing
So Far from Home
Motion Sickness: a memoir

Literary and Cultural Criticism
Armenian-North American Literature, a Critical Introduction: Genocide, Diaspora and Symbols
The Republic of Armenia and the Rethinking of the Diaspora in Literature
The Impact of the Armenian Genocide: Eighty-Three Years of Survival and Memory in the Armenian Diaspora
Survivor Memoirs of the Armenian Genocide
Quest for Closure: The Armenian Genocide and the Search for Justice in Canada
Writing Memory: The Search for Home in Armenian Diaspora Literature as Cultural Practice

The Armenian Genocide: Resisting the Inertia of Indifference (co-written with Alan Whitehorn)

The Landscape of Memory: Perspectives on the Armenian Diaspora

Under Fire: The Canadian Imagination and War (edited and wrote the introduction)

4

Restlessness

Lorne Shirinian

Blue Heron Press

Restlessness, First Canadian Edition, 2020

ISBN 978-0-920266-50-2

Blue Heron Press
502 – 1135 Logan Avenue
Toronto, Ontario
Canada M4K 3Y2

www.blueheronpress.ca

https://www.writersunion.ca/member/lorne-shirinian

For my grandsons Joshua and Aaron Gottlieb Shirinian

K. continuously had the feeling he was losing himself or had strayed further into foreign parts than anyone before him, into a foreign world in which even the air was nothing like the air at home, in which one might suffocate on the foreignness....
(Kafka, *The Castle*, 1926)

1

I had been getting progressively restless since I retired from the Department of English at McGill University five years ago. After forty years in Montreal, I needed a change, a shakeup that would give me something to look forward to in this last stage of my life. Even thinking this was frightening, this last stage of my life. Unlike most of my colleagues who couldn't wait to leave after thirty-five years in the profession and move on, I had nothing serious to attach myself to. Yes, I had colleagues but no real friends. I was divorced and had had a few unfulfilling, short-term relationships in the years since Devorah and I parted; I stayed around for another five years. Then in the middle of this last year, it became clear that I should use whatever time I had left to me more wisely. My colleagues, all much younger, gave me an appropriate send-off in our department lounge: coffee, a cake that Julie our administrative assistant had baked, a bottle of *Glen Livet* and a new *Pilot* fountain pen. Even the rector showed up to say goodbye. Everyone offered me good wishes and hoped to see me every Wednesday at the faculty club on McTavish Street across from the McLennan Library. It would have been a comfortable retirement, but my pilot light would have gone out; what remained of my imagination would have dissipated. I wanted a complete break and new challenges. I had published books and articles during my career and belonged to several academic societies and attended yearly conferences. I was most proud of the books of poetry, plays and a novel I had written during my career as my interest in academia had begun to wane some time ago. They were well reviewed, but in this country good reviews can be treacherous; they can lead you believe you have a chance to gain a larger readership and have a satisfying career and earn a living wage as an artist. It didn't take long to become disaffected by that thought then disenchanted and ultimately despondent. I spared myself that deception. I remained in the city essentially doing nothing but getting older. I fell into the habit of spending the mornings visiting the diminishing number of bookstores then having a light lunch in one of the many cafés near the university. After a short walk post lunch I would return home to nap. This wasn't at all restful as I always awoke dizzy and disoriented. After an inadequate supper, I more often than not read for a short while which usually ended up with me in tears before I would drag myself off to bed. My life had become one of purposelessness. I was swirling around the drain and had to do something quickly.

I was free and had a pension that was adequate for my limited expectations and began entertaining thoughts of continuing to work on a new novel I had started three years ago. I had sold off most of my belongings except for my favourite books, dvd's and jazz cd's and after having thought for some time about returning to Toronto, where I had lived and taught at the university until I was 30, sold my flat and put what was left of my life in Montreal in boxes and left. I had convinced myself that the time was right to focus on my novel; I would write it for me without thought of having it published. Living in a new city would give me distance from old routines. Devorah my ex-wife still lived in Toronto. After our divorce, she moved back right away, but we stayed in contact. We had decided long ago that we weren't going to have children. Our careers became our lives. Every time I think about that, I quickly fill my mind with things to avoid dwelling on it. When I emailed her, I was returning to Toronto; she said that she would be glad to have me near. I was surprised to hear that. We knew it was over between us and did our best to make her leaving as easy and amicable as possible. Sunnybrook Hospital had hired her immediately as she was a well-respected retinologist. We had been together for thirty years; it took me a long time to get over our breakup. In many ways I'm still not over it because I know it was my fault, but I'm a realist. In some ways, returning to Toronto was a homecoming; however, the city has changed so much just as I have. I've been here for four months now, and when I go downtown or to the university, I still look for my old haunts, bookstores, cafés and restaurants, but they no longer exist. Granted, there are many new ones, but the city of my youth has gone, moved on, and I haven't. I will have to spend this last portion of my life catching up and making a place for myself here. Starting anew at over seventy is stressful, but I'm hopeful as much as one can be at my age.

One morning while sipping an espresso on the terrace at *Pusateri's* at Yorkville and Bay, I started to feel a tightness in my chest. I tried to convince myself that it was nothing, a momentary discomfort, perhaps acid reflux from the coffee. I had a few colleagues who were felled by heart attacks shortly after such discomfort, so I was more than a little worried. I had tried to keep myself healthy and walked almost every day around the McGill campus and kept the same regimen here by walking around the university and the annex. I had become a vegetarian twenty years earlier and often ate Asian food in the many restaurants around the university in Montreal. That morning after the initial warning, I walked a little further but had to sit at another café on Yorkville until the pain passed. I wasn't going to be able to will this one away. I didn't want to call it angina. In the days that followed, I had similar attacks until I was no longer able to deny what might be happening. I hadn't had the chance to get a new doctor since my arrival. After some hesitation, I decided to call Devorah. She had not remarried although had had several close male friends over the years just as I had had relationships, all short lived. I wasn't certain how she would react and greet me. I took a cab home and waited for her in nervous apprehension. To my surprise, when I opened the door, she gave me a hug and kissed me on the cheek then stood back to look at me. "You're ashen," she said. "How do you feel?" I told her I still had some pain in my chest. "Right, we're going to the hospital right now," In the car, she said, "You're going to see a cardiologist. He's a friend." It's odd what one thinks of in moments of crisis. All I could focus on was her dark grey Audi A4. We hadn't seen each other for years, and all I could manage was banter about not ever bothering to buy a car since she had left. "I had no need," I said. I must have sounded balmy. I walked or took a cab everywhere I needed to go. My life was centred around the university and downtown Montreal. Since retirement, everything had become smaller and the circle tighter and tighter before I left. So instead of saying how happy I was to see her and how comfortable she seemed in her lifestyle, I blathered on. I looked over at her filled with a mixture of emotions her while she drove. We had been intimate for years then we weren't. In many ways, she was a new person, one I didn't know. I hadn't seen her for some time and was happy that she had taken care of herself. She was slender and wore her dark hair long over her bare shoulders that revealed her olive skin. Her eyes burned with an intense light as they did

14

when I had first met her. She was still the beautiful woman I had married. What had happened to us? What had I done? I had this to deal with this at the same time as I was filled with trepidation over what the doctor might find. "Don't worry," she said, "I'll help you get back on your feet." Now another rush of feelings flooded over me. She handed me two aspirins. "Here crush these and swallow." Then she handed me a small bottle. "It's nitroglycerine. Prime it by pressing down once or twice in the air away from you; then spray once under your tongue. Tell me in five minutes if the pain has subsided."

In the car, I told her I had been having shortness of breath for over two months but refused out of fear and stupidity to have a check-up. "Yesterday for the first time," I said, "I had pain in my chest."

"You know better than that. You've been in denial. You know something about that." I deserved that. She took me to the Department of Cardiology on the fourth floor of Sunnybrook Hospital and spoke quietly to the secretary who went to tell Dr. Toledano we had arrived. I knew it could be serious but tried to make light of it. He was having none of it. "You shouldn't have waited so long and at your age," he admonished. "He has always been a stubborn man," Devorah said. The doctor listened through the stethoscope then shook his head. "I've already made an appointment for a stress test with my colleague, Dr. Klein down the hall. Based on what he finds, he may send you for a nuclear diagnostic test and an angiogram. He'll see you tomorrow at nine. Here's the referral. In the meantime, no stress, no lifting. Just read and eat healthy food." Devorah has already given you some nitro. Use it if you feel anything but no more than three times then get to a hospital quickly."

On the way home, there was a tense silence I didn't know how to break. Devorah looked straight ahead at the road. I had gone from hardly any contact with my former wife or having any knowledge of her life after we split to her now being my caregiver. I was having trouble processing it all. Finally, as we neared my building, I told her how much I appreciated her help. "You probably saved my life," I said half under my breath. "Don't thank me so much. A lot can still happen." The corners of her lips were slightly upturned. She was enjoying the moment. Maybe Dr. Toledano had told her something, that it wasn't so bad, that I needn't worry, or was she having it over on me? Then I remembered I still had a $100,000 life insurance policy naming her as the beneficiary. I was starting to get angry that I hadn't changed it after all these years. Then just as I was about to get carried away with the anger, Devorah took my hand. "It'll be all right. You'll see. I'll get you through this." The kindness of strangers, I thought. I gave her hand a gentle squeeze. "Thank you," I whispered. "What was that?" she asked. "Thank you," I said louder. She was giving a little then taking it back. I was getting into dangerous territory as she pulled up to the entrance. "I'll pick you up at 8:15 tomorrow to take you to your stress test. Be ready. And remember, if you feel shortness of breath or have pain in your chest, take the nitro. If it persists, get to the hospital and call me. Come to think of it, maybe you should stay over at my place tonight just in case. Now my head was starting to spin. "Go pack a bag," she told me. "I'll wait here for you. If you're not down in twenty minutes, I'll leave." She patted me on the shoulder and said, "Go." She might as well have said, scoot or get along now. I obeyed and made sure I was back in seventeen minutes. For a few minutes at least I had forgotten about the fear burning in my chest.

In the few times we had spoken since our divorce, Devorah had never told me where she lived. "I can see you're a little lost," she said.

"I'm still not use to the city".

"It's funny how things turn out." She turned off Bayview Avenue onto Kilgour Road then left onto Burkebrook Place to her building. She pressed a button on her visor and the door to the underground parking lot opened. "I know what you're thinking. The hospital is just down the road. I often walk to work." She parked and helped me out of the car and took my bag. I followed her into the elevator and leaned against the wall. We stopped at the fifth floor then walked down the corridor to her door. I saw that the mezuzah that was on our doorframe in Montreal was now posted on the doorframe of her unit. I looked over at her, "Our mezuzah."

She inserted her key in the lock. "You obviously forgot I had taken it. I like it. It's comforting. If you want one for your place, I'll buy you one." I didn't reply.

Her condo was large, bright and modern, everything our flat near the university in Montreal wasn't. She took my bag to her guest bedroom. I smiled as my status had become "guest." This was a step up from "the ex." She came back into the living room and made sure I was comfortable then went to the kitchen. "How about some water," she said. I was dying for a coffee. "If your habits haven't changed, I know you'd like a coffee. You'd better lay off until the tests tell us more. "Water will be fine," I said. "I hope you still like eggs. I'll make us a Spanish omelet and a light salad." I told her I was looking forward to it and walked into her kitchen. She put a baguette in front of me and a bread knife. "Take the cutting board and cut some slices, please." She pointed to a scar on my index

17

finger. "Try to be careful." Years ago in our flat I nearly took my finger off trying to cut a baguette for supper after having drunk several glasses of wine. Now, I had become tentative about everything especially since the angina. I usually went about my life quietly and unobtrusively, doing what needed to be done. Here I was in an unsettling situation, and I wasn't handling myself well. "Go sit and rest. You've had a rough day. It'll be ready in fifteen minutes. You can wash up just down the hall." I came back into the living room and sat back on her sofa looking out over the green trees, the valley and beyond to Sunnybrook Hospital.

The next morning, the stress test and nuclear diagnostic test found there were blockages in two coronary arteries, one 80% blocked and a smaller artery 70% occluded. This was confirmed by an angiogram a few days later. I had to have double bypass surgery: one to my left anterior descending coronary artery and a saphenous vein graft to the posterior descending artery. It didn't sound hopeful. Because I was in danger, it had to be done quickly. For a week, I sat at home reading and watching television, trying not to get too anxious or stressed. I didn't want to end up in an ambulance with a sheet covering my face. Be calm, I told myself despite the serious and imminent danger. No exercise or straining. Every twitch in my chest made me shudder and think it was the prelude to a heart attack. A few days later, I met with the surgeon who informed me of the procedure. I was a candidate for off-pump surgery which would make post-surgery and recovery easier to handle as I wouldn't be on a heart-lung machine. The surgeon told me that there could be problems such as concentration issues and short-term memory loss as well as a slowdown of fine motor function skills and memory responses. The fact that these are usually transient leaving no permanent impairment was only of minor comfort. I couldn't get rid of the image in my mind of me sitting in a wheelchair with drool running down my chin. The next step before surgery was a meeting with a nurse at the hospital who scanned my arms and legs to find the best arteries and veins they could use for the bypasses. Things were moving quickly. Devorah insisted I stay with her until the day of the surgery. "We don't want to take a chance on something happening while you're alone." I didn't argue with her and settled in for two weeks of healthy food, reading, rest and as much relaxation possible given what I was about to go through. Most of all I enjoyed being with Devorah and talking about the old days, even going over the difficult times we had together. I didn't dare anything beyond this. She had given her time to help me through this crisis. I called her my angel of mercy. "More than you deserve, perhaps," she said. Although she had retired, she still went to her research lab a couple of mornings a week during which time I would go for a short walk in her neighbourhood then return to make a salad for us and anxiously wait for her.

One morning at the beginning of the third week, I received a call from the hospital telling me to come to the pre-surgery section this Wednesday at 6 am. This was it. Devorah took my hand. "Don't worry, Jacob; it's going to work out fine. How many of us get a second chance?"

I couldn't get it in my head that it had come to this. A second chance or…or what? I went into a deep silence. I didn't know what I should be doing in what could be my final hours. I couldn't find a word, any words. Faced with the black immensity, I had nothing, no fine phrases, finely wrought ideas. The Professor Emeritus of English Literature was unable to sum up his life and leave a profound thought, not even a touching or pathetic utterance. Here I was with my ex-wife, whom I hadn't seen for years and who had taken me in in my moment of need. I was at rock bottom before the big sleep.

"Jacob. Jacob." Devorah was pulling me out of the hole I had fallen into. I looked over to her. She saw the fear on my face. "We haven't spoken in so long; I don't know…. Do you want to speak to a rabbi?" I smiled at the thought. I hadn't been an observant Jew for so long. In the past, I always enjoyed speaking to rabbis when they weren't reaching into their bag of tricks. Most were serious and well meaning. "I thought you were going to suggest a lawyer." That angered her, but she recovered. "Let me know what you need."

"A better heart." Now I had become a smart ass.

"Why don't you lie down? I'll finish lunch."

I apologized and slouched to the bedroom. "No need to, Jacob. This is a huge moment." She came over and gave me a hug. You'll get through this." For an instant, a reflex took over, and I almost took her in my arms and kissed her, in part to thank her, in part…. I didn't want to think about that as in a short while I was going to have my chest cut open and splayed. I have to admit, though, that giving in to a moment of nostalgia would have given me an emotional bump but would have led to complications I was not ready to confront. I still carried considerable guilt over the cause of our breakup.

"Be here at 6 am; your surgery will take place at seven am." Ms. Dowson went over all I had to do before coming to the pre-op section: no food or drink, bring my medical and insurance cards, wash the night before with the surgical soap. Then she asked, "Do you have any questions?"

"Too many," I responded. There was a pause.

"Well, all right, then. We'll see you Wednesday morning. At six."

I didn't sleep for two days. I tried reading, but my mind was a scramble of thoughts and grisly images until Wednesday morning. Devorah drove me in at 5:30 and showed me where the pre-surgery registration room was. After the brief administrative formality, she sat with me while we waited to be called. "Someone will take you across the corridor to the preparation room," she said. "You'll strip; the nurse will shave your chest and give you a gown to wear. You'll wait alone until an orderly comes to take you up to the operating room." We sat in a tense silence until my name was called. I rose and Devorah put her arms around me and gave me a kiss. I was too numb to feel anything. "Good luck, Jacob. I'll be waiting for you." I kept thinking I was being led up to the gallows. Or would I prefer to be electrocuted, or shot? Time stopped. No, I'll take the lethal injection. I wanted to say "please." That's what I was thinking when the anesthesiologist plunged the catheter into the back of my right hand then shoved a needle into the connecting tube and pumped the warm liquid into me. "You'll start to feel drowsy. I'll give you the final shot in a couple of minutes." Nice choice of words, I thought. I was wheeled into the room and lifted naked onto the surgical table. The surgeon and his team were busy preparing. I was feeling warm and tingly as everything began to get blurry. "Okay, here it is, Jacob." I felt warmth streaming through my veins. I'll bring you out of it in a few hours. See you in the ICU. Now count backwards from 100." I don't know how far I got. I felt myself slip down into a dark hole.

Hours later, my eyes popped open. I felt a hand reach into my mouth and pull out a tube. Was this the other side? Someone was talking to me, but I didn't understand anything.

"Hi, Jacob. Everything is fine. Your chest is wrapped tight. Try to take deep breaths." I mumbled something and began to drift off to sleep. "No, no, we need you to stay awake." Nurses kept talking to me while they checked my vital signs. Not too long later they helped me sit up so I could dangle my legs over the side of the bed. "You'll stay in the intensive care unit till we make sure you're stable enough to go to your room." I felt as if I had a very large boulder lying on my chest. I didn't feel pain as I was full of pain killers, but there was a great pressure on my chest. "Breathe normally." I felt a hand on my cheek. "You see; that wasn't so bad, was it?" I opened my eyes wide and saw Devorah. "The surgeon told me all went well. Barring any issues, you'll be here five or six days. I'll see you every day. They're going to take you the ICU shortly."

"Five or six days," I muttered. Barring...."

"I have to go now. I'll see you tomorrow morning." She put her hand on mine then turned and left.

So that's it, then, I mumbled. I thought it would feel worse and I would end up like a bowl of jiggling strawberry jello. I looked down and saw tubes coming out of my chest. I couldn't focus on anything. There was so much pressure on my chest. One of the nurses put an extra pillow behind me and helped me sit back on the bed. I wanted to say thanks, but I drifted off with the words dissolving in my brain.

For the rest of the day, I kept going in and out of delirium and sleep. I really hadn't had much time to think of how my life had turned since my retirement. When was that? I knew it was longer than a few months, but time was playing tricks on me. I couldn't put things in any order. Chronos, why can't I? One of the nurses came to me and asked me my name. I had to think.

"Jacob."

"Do you know where you are?"

"Hospital."

"Which one?"

I could visualize the hospital but could not name it nor the street it was on.

"Do you know why you're here?"

"Heart," I mumbled.

"Where do you live, Jacob?"

That was a tough one. After so many years in the other city and being uprooted, I couldn't say.

"Don't worry. It will come back to you. I'll ask you again tomorrow. We're going to take you to your room now."

An orderly with a black patch over his right eye pushed me through the corridors into the cardiac ward and into my private room, a welcome benefit paid for after years of service at my university and taxes paid. I knew I was in for rough waters as he smacked into the doorframe rather hard twice before squeezing me through. "Shorry," was all he could manage as he sat me up and guided me onto what would be my bed for the next six days before giving me a not-so-gentle push that sent me rolling onto my back, tubes and all. "Shorry." He lifted the patch revealing a black hole where his eye used to be and the dark canal into his head. He took a breath and mumbled, "It getsh hot in there." He rearranged his patch and pushed his rolling bed straight into the doorframe once again before negotiating his way to the next victim. I wanted to laugh, but I couldn't remember how to.

I dove into a sleep and aimed straight down kicking my legs until no light shone from above. There I remained until a voice began hauling me back. "Jacob." My eyes popped open. Devorah was holding my hand. "Where were you?" she asked.

"Somewhere," was all I could manage. "It was calm. Peaceful. As if I were dead."

"Sorry to burst that bubble, but you're definitely here among us."

I was weak and confused. Devorah couldn't stay and gave my hand a gentle squeeze. "I'll see you tomorrow." My mind was barely functioning. "You'll feel better tomorrow when the effects of the anesthetic wear off. You'll eat, too."

I was wrapped tight and in pain, but the pain was subdued by pain killing medication. I knew it was there lurking just below the surface. I closed my eyes and waited for it to return, and when it became unbearable, I called for more sweet warmth in my veins. I couldn't read or do anything. I just wanted to sleep and dove back down past the hallucinations clinging to the walls, watching me, down through the depths until all went black.

Then the routine began that lasted days: morning check-up and questions, medication, breakfast, walking circles through the ward, rest and reading, mid-day checkup, lunch, more medication then more circuits with my discharge container and IV carrier, sleep, medication, another check-up then more questions followed by supper, reading and nighttime check-up and more medication then finally I could dive down once again where the thought of what I had been through and the pain disappeared for a while.

I had lost my appetite and my ability to do my bodily functions of eliminating. "Don't squeeze too hard. You don't want to burst your stitches." Finally, on the third day, I was successful. After, a nurse walked me to the shower room and stripped me down and turned a hose on me and soaped me. She handed me the cloth and told me to clean the creases then sprayed me until I felt almost normal. "You'll be going home soon," she said. I wondered where that was.

Then there was the unhooking. A male nurse with an Israeli accent, carrying a case full of scissors, gauze, clips and wraps came in and began cutting and snipping around the holes where the tubes and electric cable went into my chest then pulled them out one by one. His assistant quickly wrapped my chest up tight before any air could enter my thoracic cavity. "There. You're ready." I felt a momentary sense of freedom. "Toda," I told him. "Thanks."

He smiled. *Ata Ivrit?* Are you Jewish?" he asked in Hebrew.

I nodded. In my tender state, I was looking for a meaningful moment.

Later, I met with the pharmacist to see about all the medication I would be taking. Devorah fixed appointments with my cardiologist. And there I was, sitting in the back seat of Devorah's car being driven to her place. "You should stay with me for a few days. I want to make sure you're okay. You need to adjust to what you've been through. You have to learn how to look after yourself now."

That shocked me. I had become so used to having Devorah back in my life that I had forgotten that we led separate lives. I wanted to ask her, "You mean you're not going to look after me anymore?"

"I've arranged for a special housekeeper to come to your place every day for a number of hours until we're convinced you can live on your own again."

I knew she was right. What was I expecting? I thanked her and concentrated on not letting the bumps in the road cause me pain. I was still quite weak and sore.

That first night at her place after being discharged I was unable to remember many things. I just couldn't find the memories, names, places, people, moments. I couldn't recall anything. Over the next few days, a few memories or fragments of memories returned momentarily then disappeared again. I began to wonder if I would ever be the same. I thought that if I had lost some memories, I could create new ones. I would write them and make a novel of them unless I forgot them or forgot how.

On the third morning at Devorah's, after a particularly bad night of pain and restlessness, I was awakened by voices in the living room. I got up and went to see who was visiting. There was a man, younger than me, with his arms around Devorah. I didn't know how to react. He looked up.

"Hello, you must be Jacob." He came over to shake my hand. "I'm Dr. Michael Amar." He took my hand. "You've been through a lot, but you're in good hands."

"Michael and I worked together in Ophthalmology at the hospital."

I think I mumbled something like, "I see."

"We've been seeing each other for about six months."

"I see." Now I was feeling foolish. "You should have told me, Devorah. I wouldn't have been such a burden. You've given up so much of your time to help me. I owe you so much."

"Nonsense. You were lost and in trouble. Who else was going to save you?"

"You're an angel. Always were."

Michael went close to her and put his arms around her.

"I was going to tell you…Michael and I are leaving for a month-long trip to Europe in two days."

I swallowed hard. "That's wonderful. I'll get my things and get a cab back to my place. You must have so many things to prepare before you leave."

"Jacob, your housekeeper will begin tomorrow morning. I've given her instructions, but you should let her know what you need her to do. She is a highly specialized nurse so she'll make sure you take your medication, you walk, eat and rest as you should. I'll check in on you when we return. After three months we'll see if you still need her care."

"Thank you, Devorah. That's very thoughtful."

"Listen, this is important. If you are short of breath or in bad pain, take two of the aspirins I gave you and get to emergency quickly. Don't wait and ride it out."

I turned and returned to the guest bedroom and packed my things. Michael offered to drive me to my place, but I refused. I didn't want to hear about how their relationship had started and grew into a loving...." I took a cab back to my place. I opened the door somewhat reluctantly and looked around. Even though I had moved in months ago, it was an unfinished project like my life. The bookshelves were only half filled. Boxes of books and papers were piled in front of them. I recalled the cardiologist's warning, "Don't lift anything even moderately heavy. You need to heal." I slowly eased myself into my armchair and picked the book lying on the side table. It was good to hold a book again, but I was too tired to read. I sat back and closed my eyes. It was like starting out again. How many chances does one get?

2

That night I kept falling asleep then waking with a start only to fall back into the black cloud that had enveloped me. Finally, I was able to hold on to a dream that transported me to Salonica where my parents were born and where they always seemed to be waiting for me. Through the pain in my chest, I heard them again, telling me of their city where Sephardic Jews immigrated after being expelled from their homes in Spain by Isabella and Ferdinand in 1492 under the Alhambra Decree. Not only from pride but from knowledge gained after years of research and study, my father often said that after our expulsion, the Inquisition and exile, and from our forced journeys through Europe, we brought what we had learned, our culture, ideas, education and commerce to the city which would become our new home. "We had had a golden age in Spain when we lived there," he told me. "After our expulsion, we created another in Salonica in the 16th century. It appears that *HaShem* won't let us enjoy peace. On August 6, 1917, a huge fire destroyed a good part of the city leaving 52,000 Jews homeless. Synagogues, rabbinical libraries, schools, communal archives, businesses and clubs were all lost in the conflagration. The Jewish character of Salonica was destroyed. It was the beginning of the end for us there. In February 1943, Nazi authorities sent two specialists, Alois Brunner and Dieter Wisliceny, to carry out their genocidal plan. They immediately and vigorously applied the Nuremberg laws enforcing the display of the yellow badge and drastically restricting our freedom of movement.

"In the spring and summer of 1943, Salonica's 54,000 Jews were shipped to the Nazi extermination camps. More than 90% of the total Jewish population of the city were murdered during the war. Only the Polish Jews experienced a greater level of destruction. Even after the war, it wasn't enough. Our cemetery, the largest Jewish cemetery in Europe with over 300,000 graves dating from 1492 was appropriated by the urban planners who wanted to make the space the centre of the new Greek city of Thessaloniki. Our marble gravestones were used to rebuild the modern city." I still hear the bitterness in my father's voice. "We had to leave. How could we stay? Everything was a reminder that we weren't welcome or at home there. It was the end of La Madre de Israel."

I see my mother dressed in a white dress standing beside my father on the ship taking them away from Salonica, home, where our family had lived for centuries, never to return. He looks lovingly at my mother and takes her hand. Rose of Salonica, he calls her. "There never will be room for us," he says. "I was 28 on Black Shabbat, July 11, 1942. All the men in the community between 18 and 45 were forced into *Plateia Eleftherias*, Liberty Square, in the centre of the city where at gunpoint the Nazis forced us to do physical exercises to break our spirit and humiliate us. Many of us were then forced to do grueling road work." My father Shalom Levy a slender man, who taught French in one of the high schools was put to work in the road gang. During this time my mother was frantic, wondering if she had become a widow. The women met every day to comfort and console each other. Then some weeks later, my father did return. He just walked in the house, looking emaciated. My mother threw herself at him and wrapped her arms around him and wouldn't stop hugging him. *Mi amor*, she called him over and over. They packed and the next day left on a fishing boat for Italy where they hid for a week, sleeping by day and moving at night. In a coastal village, a kind priest helped them get on another boat moving contraband goods to Marseilles. Eventually, with the help of the French underground, they found passage to Lisbon, then Brazil and finally to America. Four and a half centuries of communal life had been destroyed. If they hadn't left, they would have been rounded up along with 54,000 of Salonica's Jews and put in the Baron Hirsch ghetto then deported to Auschwitz on March 15, 1943, on trains waiting in the station across the street. Of the few who survived the camps, some remained in Greece, in Athens, fewer remained in Salonica, which under the new Greek government had become Thessaloniki. Many went to Western Europe and America where they founded new Sephardic communities. Salonica died but was not reborn; it became something else as we did. My father settled in New York and completed his doctorate in Jewish studies, specifically in Sephardic and Ladino history, language and literature. It gave him pride after so much loss that he had dedicated himself to keeping our centuries-old culture alive. When I was young, he often told me, "You'll help me keep our history. *Zakhor*. We are commanded to remember." In New York where I was born, I would walk to the synagogue between him and my mother on Shabbat mornings and kiss her as she went to sit in the mechitzah, the women's section. I sat tight against my father and read the Torah portion with him. It was a time of such contentment, of peace like his name Shalom.

The years passed. I got my doctorate from Harvard in English literature. Although my father was sorry it wasn't in

Jewish studies, he was proud nevertheless. When I was offered a year's contract at the University of Toronto, I moved there in the late summer and began preparing my courses for the fall semester. At the train station, my parents hugged and kissed me. "This is not like leaving Salonica, Jacob. You must visit often." And I did. What followed was a series of one-year contracts that kept me in Toronto for several years, paid the bills and allowed me to ask my girlfriend Devorah to marry me. Then I won a position at McGill University in Montreal, and we moved. Devorah transferred to McGill's medical school and our lives appeared to be set. Once a month we visited Devorah's parents in Toronto; then the next month, we would go to New York. Life appeared to hold endless possibilities. But there would never be sustained peace. On a Sunday morning in December, a month before the release of his new book on the history of Ladino poetry in Salonica, my father had a heart attack and was hospitalized. My mother called, and we rushed to New York, but he died before we arrived in the city. I never had a chance to see him or speak to him again. I asked my mother to come and live with us, but she refused. All her friends and community were in New York.

It was hard returning to Montreal after the *shiva*. I had lost the taste for teaching and researching. The more I became despondent, the more Devorah applied herself to her studies in ophthalmology and became a highly sought-after researcher-practitioner, often invited to speak at conferences all over the continent.

Two years later, my mother, Rose of Salonica, passed away. I was heartbroken. They had lived through so much and had lost so much, but through persistence had managed to make a meaningful life together. Now here I was with my chest sown back together, in pain, taking awkward steps into an uncertain future. What had I hoped for from Devorah in the city where we married so many years earlier? She saved my life. She was too kind to bring up the issues we had had together in the past and which ultimately broke us apart. I feel that she honoured our time together by saving me.

I awake searching for a breath. I put my hand on my chest and feel the long, red scar that is painful to the touch. I close my eyes and see my mother in her white dress on the ship taking them away from Salonica. My father puts his arm around her as they lean into the sunlight together. I need a perfect moment, something that will erase some of the past, something that will offer some hope to this dream I'm living.

3

From across the ocean, I hear my name floating over the waves. My parents are calling me. Jacob. Jacob. Against the morning sun pouring in through the living room windows, I see her silhouetted. "Jacob. Jacob Levy."

"Mmm," I attempted a response.

"Jacob. I'm Mrs. Ben Soussan. Devorah arranged for me to care for you until you can look after yourself." Before I could ask how she got in, she said, "Devorah had a key made for me. I hope you don't mind me coming into your bedroom. It's best not to be so formal in these circumstances."

"Yes, of course. I'm sorry. I was somewhere else. What time is it?"

"7:30 am. We should talk and establish a routine. I'll cook and clean and make sure you take all your medication. We'll go for walks, and I'll accompany you to all your medical appointments."

All I could do was thank her. I rose rather unsteadily and offered her my hand.

"Please call me Abby, and I'll call you Jacob. Agreed?"

"Agreed."

"Have you eaten yet?"

"No, I should."

"Have you had your morning meds?"

"No."

"Show me where they are then."

She put all my medication bottles in order and made a timetable for when I should take each pill and how many."

"Only decaf coffee for the next six months. Devorah told me you hadn't been home for a while so I did a little shopping to get you started. I didn't get you any decaf though. I'll bring some tomorrow."

"Please make sure it has lots of flavour."

"I will. Have you showered yet?

"No."

"Do you need help?

"I can manage," I told her.

"Call me if you need me. Remember to do everything slowly. I'll make us a veggie omelet with slices of toast and light cheese."

That's how it began. I could hear her puttering in the kitchen as I turned on the tap and let the warm water run in rivulets down my chest and pulled the soapy cloth carefully over my body. I turned a slow circle, holding on to the safety bars I had installed before moving in. Everything still hurt. I rinsed the soap away then turned off the water and stepped gingerly out of the stall and stood naked before the mirror. Not much to look at. But I'm alive.

I sat at the table with Abby, and we ate together. While I drank herbal tea, she helped herself to my dark roast coffee. She smiled as she drank it, knowing full well what I would do for some.

"You'll have coffee tomorrow, Jacob. Sit and read for a bit; then we'll go for a walk." She was firm but warm in her own way that I couldn't say was endearing.

"I'm tired."

"Of course, you are. But we have to get all your muscles working, especially your heart. You need to expand your lungs."

"Devorah told me you were a nurse."

"In Israel during the '67 and Yom Kippur Wars."

"When did you leave?"

"My husband was killed on the Golan in '73. I stayed until 1980.

"Why did you leave?"

"I felt everything was closing in. There was a lot of guilt in leaving, but the time was right for me to go. I went to stay with family in Paris.

"You're from France, then?"

"My parents were; they made *aliya* when they returned from the camps after the war. I grew up in Israel then spent ten years in France. I immigrated to Canada in 1990 as France was becoming more and more anti-Semitic. I had developed skills as a field hospital trauma nurse that I taught here. That's how I met Devorah at the hospital."

"Do you know Dr. Amar?" I asked sharply.

"We've met."

"What do you think of him?"

"You mean how does he treat Devorah?

I nodded.

"He loves her. She loves him. After what you've just been through together, you don't want to hear this."

"We've been separated for 10 years."

"We should walk."

The spring air was wonderful. I took deep breaths even though each lungful was painful as the doctor had deflated my left lung to have better access to my heart then inflated it after the surgery. My whole left side hurt.

Abby kept me at a slow but steady pace on the uneven sidewalks. I had the chance to look at her closely in the morning light. She was perhaps 5 feet 5 or 6 inches tall, with deep penetrating, dark eyes and was slender and shapely. She was likely in her mid 60's. Her long, dark, straight hair fell on her shoulders. She wore no makeup and dressed modestly though in a modern way. We were probably born only five or six years apart, but I felt so much older, as if I had lost pieces of my life along the way and even memories of what I had been. I could see how she could have led a trauma team under fire.

"Were you born into an orthodox family, Abby?"

"Yes. Now you're going to ask why I left. Not today, please. We don't know each other well enough. Besides, it's an old story for me that likely wouldn't impress a writer-professor like you."

"Like me?"

"Devorah gave me a copy of your novel to read."

"No comments, please. We don't know each other well enough. Let's just walk."

She checked her watch. "That's 35 minutes. It's a good start. We'll do 45 tomorrow. She smiled and upped the pace slightly, enough for me to trip over a crack in the sidewalk. "Careful," she said and slid her arm under mine to steady me and kept it there. I was tired and needed to rest.

"You must let me know if at any time you feel dizzy or have trouble breathing."

Climbing back from the edge wasn't going to be easy. "I'm okay," I told her.

"You'll see; each day, you'll feel a little better. I'll be here with you."

For the first time since my surgery that felt comforting.

I went to my writing room and sat at my desk and opened the manuscript of the novel I had been working on before leaving Montreal. As I flipped through the pages, it was clear that there were more sentences scratched out than had remained untouched. I had titled it *Final Resting Place*, rather ironic given what has happened to me here. Nevertheless, completing this work was important to me as were all the projects I had begun. I turned to my notebook and read the quote from Herman Hesse's essay in *My Belief: Essays on Life and Art* that I had written down.

Among the many worlds which man did not receive as a gift of nature, but which he created with his own mind, the world of books is the greatest. Every child, scrawling his first letters on his slate and attempting to read for the first time, in so doing, enters an artificial and complicated world; to know the laws and rules of this world completely and to practice them perfectly, no single human life is long enough. Without words, without writing, and without books there would be no history, there could be no concept of humanity. And if anyone wants to try to enclose in a small space in a single house or single room, the history of the human spirit and to make it his own, he can only do this in the form of a collection of books.

This was my belief throughout all my years as a professor and has remained so as a writer who is perhaps working on his final book. I need to have the health and strength to complete it.

4

Three weeks ago, I never would have believed that I would be able to walk for fifty-five minutes in the neighbourhood at a reasonable pace and not be fatigued. My left side was still quite sore, and I suffered from pains in my neck and shoulders, but I actually looked forward to the exercise. Before the surgery, when I walked, I surrounded myself with an invisible wall that kept me apart from everyone. Since her arrival, Abby has always taken my arm whenever we go out together. Gradually, her guidance though still firm became softer; I want to say sweeter. The test to see if my respiration was improving was the ability to maintain a conversation while we walked. I could remember things in my past without too much trouble; however, what happened yesterday or a month ago often escaped me. I could recall specific moments while recovering in the hospital but not much more other than the general sensation of pain and awkwardness as I tried to rediscover my life. I began dreaming more and more about my mother and father. "Be patient," Abby told me, "things will return to you. Focus on getting better; the rest will follow."

One sunny morning before breakfast, I went to shower while Abby prepared my medication. As the hot water ran down my body, I began to feel weak. A strong wave of fatigue ran through me, causing my right knee to buckle, sending me crashing on the tiled floor. I must have called out because Abby came rushing in and turned off the water. "Don't try to get up right away. Are you dizzy?" I told her I wasn't. "Are you in pain anywhere?" I shook my head. She rolled me over on my side and put her arm around me and helped me up. We stood facing each other. "Here, lean on me. Can you stand?" She moved closer and held me then reached over to get my towel and wrapped it around my midsection then took another one and began drying me. She walked me to the bed and helped me lie down. "Just rest for a while." She began inspecting the stitches down my chest to make they hadn't pulled open. They hadn't. She then lifted the towel from my thigh to check my knee. "It's a little red but not swollen. Can you move it?" I moved it around. "It's a little painful," I told her. "Just relax. I'll get you up shortly. You should eat. We'll try walking tomorrow." I was observing me observing her as she was taking care of her patient. She took a blanket from the linen closet and covered me. Her hands went under and removed the wet towel around me and put it in the laundry. When she returned, she stretched out on the bed next to me. "Just breathe naturally, Jacob. Close your eyes. This was a lesson, a warning. We have to slow down, proceed more carefully."

For a time, I lived in the rhythm of the throbbing pain in my knee. Abby lay still, but I could hear her quiet breaths. Then she spoke almost in a whisper. "I was with a forward combat field hospital close to the front line in the Golan. There was a constant stream of helicopters, ambulances and trucks bringing in our wounded. We had just sewed up a teenager with a through and through in his chest. I was about to change gloves for the next soldier, when one of my colleagues, the triage nurse, pulled me aside. 'Abby,' she said, 'come, it's Alon.' I went numb as I followed her to the triage tent. Alon, my husband of 3 years was lying on stretcher with thick layers of gauze wrapped tightly around his neck. We pulled back the bandages and found that part of his neck had been shot away; he was bleeding out rapidly. I got more gauze and wrapped it tightly around the wound, but there was nothing to be done. I hugged him and stayed with him until one of the doctors came and checked him and pronounced him dead. There was no time to mourn him at that time. There was simply too much to do. I went back into the operating theatre and did my job helping those who might be saved. Alon, killed on the Golan in 1973."

I moved my hand towards her until I touched her hand and held it. "I know a few things about dying, Jacob. You have a lot to live yet. I promised Devorah I would help you. Let's sleep a while; then we'll see about your knee."

Sometime later, I'm not sure how long, Abby came in and sat on the bed beside me. "I've made us a lunch." She pulled the blanket down off my chest and ran her hand over me. "I noticed this when I helped you from the shower." Her finger skated along the 5-inch scar below my ribs on the left side. "I've seen many of these. Were you shot?"

"It happened a long time ago," I told her.

"It appears to have healed well."

"The flesh healed, but not so much the mind. I was 17. My parents went ahead to the synagogue for Shabbat services. I followed a little later. I took a shortcut through some side streets and was stopped by a group of four kids about my age. 'Hey, Jew boy,' they called out. I just kept walking, but they followed and surrounded me. Then they began pushing me around, taunting me the whole time. I tried to run, but one of them tripped me. Then a flurry of kicks and punches followed. I managed to get up and threw punches in the air that caught one of them in the face. He fell down. 'Jew bastard,' they cursed. 'Now you're going to get it.' I saw the sun glint off a blade one of them held. He started jabbing at me. I moved to avoid being hit, but he lunged at me. I managed to put my tallit bag in front of it, but it went through and into my flesh. They ran away. I crawled out to 70th street where people helped me and called an ambulance. The blade just missed my spleen. The wound healed, but I didn't." She continued gently rubbing the scar.

"It's what we have to endure."

"I'll never forget it."

"You must be hungry. Can you get dressed?"

I nodded.

"Come to the kitchen when you're ready." She got up and went to plate a light lunch. I ran my finger over the scar, but all I felt was Abby's hand.

During the first month at home after the bypass, I continued to make progress; I was not, however, able to put names to faces, or faces to names. Words I had used regularly became eclipsed in the thick fog shrouding my memory. Just this morning in conversation with Abby, I had the meaning of the word I wanted to use to mean insincere, dishonest, or deceitful but could not find the word other than I was certain it began with the letter "d." Try as I might, it escaped me and plagued me for most of the day until I heard an announcer use it on the 7 o'clock news, saying "disingenuous," referring to the American president. A part of my life had now become the search for words and names to describe the world and people around me. If my surgery had made clear the impermanence of my life, the inability to use language was yet another indication that I had reached the point of losing chunks of what I had been. My general health was improving, but I felt I was losing myself. Yes, I was a professor and maybe even a writer of sorts, but under the circumstances, what does being a wise man mean?

I had forgotten that every moment, each step I take involved making a choice. There were times when walking on Bloor Street near Avenue Road that severe anxiety would suddenly fill me. It wasn't because I was going to walk out into the heavy noonday traffic, but rather that I couldn't trust myself that I wouldn't. Kierkegaard's idea that anxiety is the dizziness of freedom was so right. How ironic. I had taught the existentialists for a number of years. It's one thing to read about it in a literary text, quite another to live the dangers of freedom firsthand. I had survived heart surgery and was recovering. I had so much to look forward to, so much to live for, Abby would say. So why did I feel as if I were living my life on the edge of a precipice?

In the evenings, I had begun to help Abby prepare our supper. At first, she didn't want me to, but then she saw it as part of my recovery and gave me more and more kitchen tasks. I would stand beside her and peel carrots. Our bare arms touched lightly as we worked, neither moving to create more space between us. During supper last night I mentioned that I was writing a new novel that the bypass interrupted. I wondered out loud if I would find the ideas and energy to pick it up again. "The future is important, more so than the past. All that you're doing is making a difference. You have to keep moving forward, creating." She was right; it's what the existentialists wrote, that existence and action are a choice, a form of self-assertion. "Jacob, you should throw yourself into your own life; affirm every moment." She was right, but I had to find my life through the pain and thick fog that still enveloped me.

One night after a full afternoon of walking and food shopping, we came back to my place and cooked a vegetarian pasta meal. We sat on the couch and watched the depressing news. Abby filled a second glass of wine for herself. With all the medication I was taking, I wasn't going to risk anything by drinking alcohol. We nestled in and surfed through the channels. Abby laid her head on my shoulder. I took the glass from her and put it on the side table. I could feel the warmth of her body and hear her gentle breaths. I began to think about it and became confused. We remained close next to each other for a time. At 10 pm I rose and got a blanket and a pillow. I took her shoes off and helped her stretch out on the couch and covered her. "Good night," I whispered and went to the bedroom and lay down on the cover, closed my eyes and tried to dream.

But I was unable to. Neither my students nor colleagues appeared. The flat Devorah and I shared came to me along with the wonderful times we had spent there when we were younger. I lingered for a while on this; then the fights and her decision to leave, and I wished I hadn't wandered there. I remember as a young boy the nights at our home in Manhattan, being with my mother and father. It was so warm. It felt safe. I knew the world outside was not always what my scar showed me it could be. I wondered if they had felt the same about their home in Salonica, the haven for Sephardic Jews that in the end was not. I felt nostalgia, a longing to return home, a yearning for a different time, but there wasn't a home to return to, nor was there a time when things were different. I wondered, lying here with stiches down my chest from the bypass surgery, if they were better. Most of my life, I always dealt with the here and now. I felt powerless, no longer able to create effects that

43

would transform my life. I had become what I had been thinking for some time: retired, damaged, divorced, an old Jew having nothing important left to say if indeed I ever had. Surely in all my years as a professor, I made a difference to some. I need to believe that. I don't know anymore. Whole portions of my life have vanished. Every now and then, I get a flash, an image which even though it disappears instantly, teases me as if its chemical tentacles in that instant attempt to link and lead to another. The other day I heard Miles Davis's *All Blues*. I sensed there were associations with the song, parts of my past, but I couldn't piece it together.

Then there is Abby. The fall weather had arrived bringing cooler temperatures, wind and rain. One night, Abby asked me if she could stay the night as it was too miserable outside. Of course, I welcomed her. I helped her make a bed on the couch. It was comforting waking up, knowing she was here. It was more than that. Some days later, I surprised myself by asking her if she wanted to stay. The quizzical look on her face indicated she needed a clarification. "I mean move in." It was hard to believe. She took my hand and asked, "Are you sure, Jacob?" I didn't know anything about her life outside the bubble of our relationship, where she lives, whether she lives alone. She took my hand. "Yes," she said. "Yes, I will." I told her that we could bring her things over. She looked me straight in the eyes and asked pointedly, "Are you sure you want to do this? I gently put my arms around her, "I want us to be together. Things will be difficult, my age and health." She smiled, "Not to worry;" she joked, "we'll get a wheelchair for you tomorrow." I tried saying something but only ended up stuttering. Abby laughed, "If I get bored, I'll give you two-days' notice before leaving." All I could manage was, "Deal." As I had lost parts of my life, I had chosen now to live in the here and now. What I couldn't recover with Abby, I would invent. For the first time, she held me close and kissed me.

5

Every day I hung on to her for dear life until one day, something in me became unblocked. We walked together with greater energy and purpose. I was healing, transforming, and it felt wonderful. We continued preparing meals together. After supper we would stretch out on the couch and read. When we tired, we went to bed. I hadn't slept so well in years. I forgot about my heart. I was less glum about life. I was evolving, becoming a new and better person. But it was hard changing old habits. Abby never criticized me when I fell back into my old ways. After living alone in my flat in Montreal after Devorah left, surrounded by my books, music and manuscripts, and taking daily walks in a city that was more and more closing in on me, it would take time and effort. I changed because I wanted to make my remaining years hopeful and if possible, meaningful. Even my writing changed. I was most comfortable with existential anti-heroes. It was my natural stance that years of experience had ingrained in me. I believed it, lived it, and teaching it reinforced the vision. No matter how much I wonder about the meaning of life and how many questions I ask, in the end, they always come tumbling back down. The paradox of needing to ask ultimate questions and the impossibility of receiving an adequate answer is the essence of the absurd. Finding a new optic and a new language would take time.

It had been about 3 months since Devorah had left on her extended vacation. I hadn't heard from her and thought she might have moved on now that she had saved me. Then one morning she knocked at the door. When I opened it, she stood before me tanned and beautiful. I just looked at her, smiling until she asked, "Well, can I come in?" Somewhat embarrassed, I took her hand, "Sorry. Of course. Thank you for coming over. I was wondering when I would see you again." She entered and looked around. "Abby has done wonders."

"What, you don't think I could have maintained some order?"

"My recollection of your habits is different. And besides, you've been through a lot."

I smiled and confessed. "You're right though. Abby has turned my life around. I owe it all to you, Devorah."

"I think Abby deserves all the credit. We've been talking to each other. I knew she was the one, Jacob. You appear to be recovering well. I dare to say you look happy."

This was not a term I used to describe myself, but in my way I was. I told her that Abby was out shopping but should return soon. "Would you like some coffee?"

She thought for a moment then said, "I can't stay. I don't know if Abby has spoken to you, but I found Abby a job at the hospital in emergency."

She hadn't mentioned it to me. I was happy for her. I knew her skills could be used to save people.

Devorah walked towards the door and turned. "She's very talented. Treat her kindly, Jacob."

"And you," I asked. "How's Michael?"

"I wasn't sure how to tell you this. We got married in Israel."

I don't know why, but I wasn't prepared to hear this. I leaned forward and kissed her cheek. "*Mazal tov*. I wish you both well."

She took my hand. "Thank you. It's strange, isn't it?

"It is," I admitted.

"Stick to your schedule. It has to be a life-long commitment if you want to live longer."

Before leaving, she wished Abby and me the best. I closed the door behind her and sat on the couch and went over my life with Devorah, at least what I could remember of it and thought of my life with Abby. I was a lucky man to have both in my life.

Abby was happy to return to the hospital to train emergency room nurses. Her day started early. While she showered, I prepared breakfast for her for which she never failed to thank me with a kiss. Then she was out doing good in the world while I, after showering, sat at my desk and went over what I had written the day before, hoping that the new day would bring more clarity and sense to what I was trying to accomplish. It wasn't always so. Some days, after reading several pages, I closed the leather cover on the manuscript and got up dejected. Asking myself, "Where the hell am I going with this?" had become a daily ritual. Then there were other days, when what I had written made sense and pointed to future action, ways forward for my characters to take that pushed the plot forward and took the story in a new and exciting and sometimes scary direction, daring me to follow. I was on to something. In my mind I began thinking of myself a writer and not the old professor of English literature who had retired and run out of ideas. Every morning I couldn't wait to get to my desk and open the manuscript and take the cap off the Dupont Orpheo fountain pen in deep blue lacquer that Devorah had bought for me years ago after my first novel was published. "For the next one," she said. There never was a next one I was happy with. Except that now I was certain there would be, and I wouldn't stop until there was. I would dedicate it to Devorah and Abby, who saved my miserable life. Yes, there were more bad days writing than days that illuminated my future. I realized that the effort, the doing, was everything. I would continue until I felt I was close to finishing it then would send it off to a publisher for the crapshoot random casino roulette, three-card monte, step forward and take your chance life lotto if you don't have a ticket, you can't win. So few win no matter how good the writing is.

At the beginning of the following week, I decided to go downtown and visit a couple of used bookstores, something I hadn't done since my surgery. I missed leafing through old books. Sometimes pulling open the cover of a dry paperback would crack the spine leaving certain pages free of the chronological tyranny of the particular story. In rare anarchic moments, I would reshuffle the pages or exchange them with pages from another novel that had also freed itself from plot and story line. As much as I enjoyed used bookstores, I now suffered from the dust and odors of literature decaying on the shelves. After 20 minutes of sneezing and watery eyes, I cradled 6 titles in my arms to give them a new home. I walked slowly along the row of shelves holding fiction in an approximation of alphabetical order. In the "S" section, a title caught my attention. *No Other Country, No Other Shore* by Jacob Levy. There I was, not in alphabetical order and on the wrong shelf, my name having faded away after years of sitting unopened and unclaimed in the sun that forced its way in through the dirty front window. I took the book from the shelf and opened it. I was amazed to see that the last book I had published before retiring and leaving Montreal had somehow emigrated to Toronto as I had. Diaspora Press had published the book then soon after closed its doors. No doubt the name of the press should have warned the brave publisher of the fate of his endeavor. I was never informed of the closure or what happened to the remaining stock of my book. The author and his book had disappeared except for this chance trace of their existence. I wondered who could have purchased the book? Who might have brought it to Toronto then abandoned it in the used bookstore?

I purchased the books then walked to a café a few doors down. I needed an espresso and a little time to breathe and look over my book before heading home. Was the world trying to send me a message? Which one? Your books will be discarded and abandoned. Or your books will be passed on around the world through generations. As I never wrote with the idea of making money from my books, I liked both messages, that the fortune of books is similar to that of people. Holding my book offered me yet another moment of self-reflection. I sat back with my espresso and tasted the dark liquid, which always made me feel good then opened the thin volume that either protested or welcomed me with a loud CRACK which set the pages free. I sat back and shuffled the loose pages, and as I looked over each one, the words came alive and took me back to the time I wrote the book when Devorah and I were still together, and the future was to be won. I never worried about time; there was always enough, I thought, to make things right.

I had dedicated the book to my parents. Their fate as diaspora Jews was always a present reality in my life. Although I was born in America and lived more than half of my life in Canada, I felt it too. I was never a Jew in the way my mother and father were. After so many centuries, it must be a genetic condition for us in the sense that the Greeks meant it, pathos meaning suffering and ology meaning the study of. More precisely in this context, it describes abnormal conditions that can for some feel like a disease. Most Jews I know are afflicted in some way. The smart ones let it go, shift gears and change lanes at high speed. But how can one leave one's past? Even at speed, it's always in the rearview mirror. I tried many times; then when you're absorbed in something else, you raise your head, and there it is, a word, a phrase, an image or a memory. Wherever I am, if I begin to feel comfortable, I get nervous, restless. That's my condition. As I reread my novel after so many years, it became clear this is what I was exploring. I reread a portion of the introduction.

No Other Country, No Other Shore. Our myths have been displaced. We wander mystified in search of them in new cities where they wait for us.

Lost again. This time in Montreal where the streets wind like an angry noose to a dead end. You told us we'll go to another country, another shore. We'll find another city. Whatever we do is fated to turn wrong.

You said we'll go to another country, to another shore. But cities always pursue us: these same streets and neighbourhoods. Don't hope for elsewhere. There are many ships and many roads but no elsewhere, only the home lost. There's no new country, no new shore, only these cities that will always pursue us.

Here, adrift on the indifferent streets, I am no longer certain of what I was. But vague memories. Now desire lies across my body like an open wound.

Lost. Through the mysterious roads I am drawn.

There is so much time to mourn one's fortune. So much uncertainty. So much work gone wrong. Deceptive plans. Say good-bye to home forever. Don't fool yourself; don't think it is a dream.

At home, she lay in the sweet grass, her naked legs draped over the bank, floating free in the Aegean. The gold of the sun spilled across the water and over her expectant body. A warm breeze rustled the stalks around her. In the clear blue sky high above, fear plowed a furrow through the buzzing of bees and cicadas. Her golden legs dangled; her arms lazily moved across her belly; her hands cupped her breasts.

By the rivers of Babylon we sat and wept when we remembered Zion. There on the poplars we hung our harps, for there our captors asked us for songs, our tormentors demanded songs of joy; they said, "Sing us one of the songs of Zion!"

On that day when the ship took her away and home disappeared into memory, her tears flowed out past the city and dissolved into the ocean.

Now, years later, she wonders if there is anyone at home who will remember her and hope she's alive.

I can see how screwed up I was then. It's taken a lot of years and pain to deal with the loss of my parents and their loss. It never goes away. And then I lost Devorah through my willful stupidity, something I've refused to confront all these years. Now a few short months ago, I almost lost my life. I must be leading a charmed existence because I've found Abby. Truthfully, it was Devorah, who found her for me. Finding such a person at my age is more than I deserve; it's almost enough to make me an optimist. The other night, I told Abby I loved her. It was the first time. She looked at me unsure of how to respond. She put her hand on my cheek and kissed me and whispered, "And I." She nursed me back from the edge. How could I not?

6

One morning after Abby had left for the hospital, I found myself dancing around the living room. Something had happened when I got out of bed. The immense weight that had oppressed me physically and mentally that had rendered my every step tentative and had made me dizzy and off balance had suddenly disappeared six months after my surgery. My chest was still sore as were my shoulders, but I could cope with that. I knew the pain would eventually disappear. Being dizzy and off balance were still worrisome, but that morning I sensed that the problems were waning. I tested my new self by dancing and whirling around the room as if I were waltzing with Abby. Apart from a slight collision with a floor lamp, I was still standing and could walk through entranceways without banging into the doorframes. There was no doubt about it; I was feeling better. I needed to write.

I made a decaf espresso. Yes, I had decided to take it easy on my arteries and heart and stick with decaf. I went to my writing desk and opened the manuscript. I checked the ink supply in my Dupont and began. There was energy behind the word flow. I didn't even bother to reread passages; there would be time later. Unconscious, I went where it took me. I wrote.

Sometime later I became aware of the sunlight that had entered the room as it did every morning shortly before noon. Almost two hours had passed. I reached for the cup and sat back and let the last cold drops of coffee drip into my mouth.

Twelve pages. I had written twelve pages. I gathered them and put them in my knapsack. I needed to walk before going over them.

After a brisk 45-minute saunter, I found myself in front of Waterman's Bookstore Café near the university close to the *Harbord Bakery*, where I would often go when I was a young lecturer here so many years ago. As the lunch crowd had returned to the campus, I sat at a table by the front window. The walls surrounding me were filled with new and used books. There were only a few customers reading and writing at the tables around me. I took out the manuscript and my pen and looked around before getting down to work. At the table next to mine was a man in his mid to late 30's, working rather intensely on a thick sheaf of paper. The title page lay separated from the rest on which he had placed his cup of coffee, *After Hannah*. The inclusion of the "h" at the end of the word was interesting. One of the tribe I speculated. If so, it would mean after grace. Atheist or not, we're all looking for some kind of grace in this world. I thought of Abby and how her hands were likely inside someone's bloody chest cavity while I was sipping yet another coffee, pen in hand gliding over this story, an account of past events in my life I was trying to give meaning to, looking for mercy, a reprieve, wondering if it's the evolution of something or the end. I just need a little more time to love and be loved. I just want the story to end well. Why do I always fear the worst?

I worked for about 90 minutes thickening out the story line and introducing new characters until a student with a knapsack on her back turned sideways to get by the table next to mine and brushed some sheets from my neighbour's manuscript onto the floor. I leaned over to gather them and handed them back. "Thanks," he said, and placed them back on the pile. "I see you're afflicted too," I said wondering who *After Hannah's* author might be. He didn't respond right away until he looked at the pile of sheets on my table. "Yes," he said. "It's a self-inflicted wound." He stuck out his hand, "Jake Calman." I shook his hand, "Hi Jake, I'm Jacob Levy. I'm going to have another coffee, can I get you one?" I could see that he was a rather intense person, but I was looking for something, a paragraph I could add to the day's page. He looked hardened, angry and even bitter, but he was writing with a vigour that intrigued me.

I returned with two cups of espresso and placed them on our tables. I looked up and saw a man about my age sitting in the corner near us. He was a little shorter perhaps, balding, huddled over his thick notebook, working the nib of his fountain pen, a *Danitrio Cum Laude* in blue celluloid. He looked up and smiled over to us; I returned the smile. He put his head down and continued writing. I liked this place; there was a very good vibe conducive to literary work.

"Are you working on a novel?" I asked Jake. "Been writing this one for over three years." I asked him how close he was to finishing. "I don't think I'll ever finish it." The person in the corner was within earshot of our conversation. His pen was writing furiously. I turned my attention back to Jake. Perhaps I was being too bold, but I asked him, "Who is Hannah?" He leaned back in his chair and sighed. "She was my wife. I'm trying to put down what happened, but…even as I'm writing it, it sounds unbelievable." I took a sip of the rich, dark liquid. "Are you writing it for publication or for yourself?" He picked up a stack of sheets. "I've only had one novel published, and that was a few years ago. I'm ready for another one. Maybe seeing it out on the shelves will help me get over what happened." I asked him if anyone had read his manuscript yet;

he shook his head. I'm not ready for that." He finished his coffee and thanked me and put everything in his bag. "I'll be here tomorrow morning, Jacob. If you're here, I'll tell you the story if you're interested." I told him I was and that I would meet him at the café the next morning. We shook hands and said goodbye. I wondered if he was going to show up tomorrow. I worked for an hour or so longer. The writer in the corner sat back and stretched his arms over his head as if he had just accomplished something satisfying. He closed his notebook, and as I readied to leave and got up, he said, "The work never stops. See you tomorrow."

7

After breakfast the next morning, I kissed Abby goodbye before she left for the hospital. I sat at my desk and wondered whether I should return to the café and meet with Jake Calman and see the quiet man who was sitting in the corner filling his notebook. He was a quiet one, yet I wanted to know more about him as he seemed to know what was going on around him at the café, the various writers and their stories. I packed my manuscript and my pens and set out. When I got to Bloor Street, I got a call from Abby. "Are you okay, Jacob?"

"Yes," I told her, "Why?"

"You've been different the past few days."

"I'm sorry; I hadn't noticed."

"That's what I mean," she said.

I told her that having lived alone for a long time, I had gotten used to doing things without paying much attention to —."

"Me," she said.

"You're right. When I'm in a writing mode, I tend to block things out to concentrate on the work."

"I understand," she said. "I'm not used to seeing you like this."

"You mean you prefer me as a patient."

The moment I said it, I knew I had stepped in it. She went silent. I apologized again. "That was stupid, Abby. Forgive me."

"Why did you say it, then, Jacob?"

"I guess I'm a little confused. This story I'm writing is actually good; it has a chance of getting published. I'm not use to things going well. I'm always waiting for the other shoe to drop."

"Like now," she said.

"Yes. You see, it always does."

"Look, my love, go write, feel good about what you're doing. We'll talk tonight. I'm a little stressed too. They're bringing in a family who was in an accident on the 401. It sounds bad."

"Abby, they're lucky to have you looking after them." Silence. I told her I loved her.

"I love you, too. I need to hear it more often, Jacob. I have to go prep."

No matter what I would write that day, it wouldn't come close to being as important as what Abby was about to do for that family. I arrived at the café and found that the table by the window I had sat at yesterday was free. I sat and looked around. Jake wasn't here yet. I unpacked my manuscript, but I wasn't sure I even wanted to unscrew the cap off my Mont Blanc 149. I just sat there going over my conversation with Abby. Living alone for so long had given me a great deal of freedom. But also loneliness. I had to learn to be considerate to a partner again. My time with Abby was a rehabilitation in becoming a better man.

"Not sure Jake is coming today." I looked over to the man at the corner table. He put his pen down. "I'm Lorne." He got up and came over to me and extended his hand. "Mind if I sit for a while?" I shook his hand and pulled out a chair for him. "I know Jake well. He hasn't been the same since his kidnapping."

"He was kidnapped? Here in the city?"

"Right here."

He flexed his hand. "Writer's cramp. I've been at it since early this morning. When the words come, you have to give in to the energy. Most of the time, we just push words around hoping for connections, hoping they're like little binoculars that allow you to look ahead to what might be there. Since yesterday, I can see where it's going, where I'm going."

I nodded.

"Getting back to Jake…if you like, I can tell you his story. He won't mind; he tells everybody. I think one day he'll actually write the story and sell it. It'll never bring him peace though."

Lorne appeared to be a quiet, introspective person. Looking at him in the corner hunched over this manuscript and notebooks with a bunch of fountain pens in a leather pouch ready for action, I never would have guessed he wanted to talk. I wasn't in the mood to get into my story so soon after the phone call. I needed to listen for a while. "Sure, Lorne," I told him, "I'd like to hear it. Let me get us some coffee first."

"Decaf espresso for me, please," he said.

I returned with two cups and sat.

"I've known Jake for at least six years. I met him at a writer's conference at Harbour Front. He was the typical university graduate who wanted to be a writer, stressed and obsessed, uncertain about whatever idea he had or story he had written. Nevertheless, he managed to get his first novel published, *Looming Threat*, a crime story. It received a few good reviews, but like most first novels in this country it had a short run and was soon remaindered. He began working on a second novel without any success. Fortunately, his wife, Hannah, worked in information technology downtown and could pay the bills. Jake worked in a bar on Bayview near Millwood Road called *Bottoms Up*. He did everything from cleaning, stocking the shelves, to bar tending and bouncing. It was this last part of his job description that got him in trouble. As I said, Jake was going through a tough time with his novel and was feeling rather undervalued as Hannah was the breadwinner, although having talked to her, I know she never said anything to him to make him feel inadequate. They were a solid couple. Nevertheless, Jake had an enormous chip on his shoulder. One night a rough group came into the bar near closing time. One obnoxious lout got surly when Jake refused to serve him past closing. A fight broke out. Jake channeled all his frustration on the guy and clobbered him, humiliated him. The guy left swearing revenge. Now Jake and Hannah lived on Manor Road, not far from the bar. On the way home late that night, the guy and his two friends ambushed Jake and pulled him into their car and roughed him up. They were a small-time crew of criminals, robbery and extortion mostly. The guy he beat up wanted to kill Jake and throw him over the Scarborough Bluffs. The other two said no. Now that they had let themselves be convinced by their friend to beat up Jake, they didn't know what to do. So they kidnapped Jake and in time took him on all the petty robberies they committed. At night they chained him to a pipe in a small warehouse where they hid out. Jake told me that there was a point when he actually joined their gang. Here's the sad part for Jake. The gang would often drive over to his place and watch Hannah through the large living room window. The lead detective on his kidnapping got friendly with Hannah as there had been no word from Jake, no trace of him for almost 2 years. In the end, he moved in with her. Jake could do nothing because in order to escape from the gang, he had to kill. He did away with two of them but not the leader, Al, I think his name was. He couldn't reclaim his wife without the detective asking questions and possibly finding out about the murders. Jake has been writing *After Hannah* since then. I don't think he'll ever finish it. Sometimes I go with him and park in front of his old place on Manor Road. We look at Hannah and her detective husband. I tell him he has to move on. I don't know what he's going to do. Honestly, I've thought about writing his story with embellishments. I even began writing a film script about it."

"That's quite a story, Lorne."

As we continued talking for almost an hour, customers came and went. Some came over to say hello to Lorne and ask how the new story was coming along. "Having a good day," he would say," and they would pat him on his shoulder.

"I'm curious," he said. "What is there in your life, Jacob, that would make a cracking story?"

"Cracking. I'm not sure. I'm still trying to work it out. For some time now health issues have clouded everything I do." We talked some more; then at noon, he wrote something in his notebook then packed up his things. "I hope to see you here again," he said. "I look forward to hearing how your project is coming along. Twenty minutes after he left, I headed back to our place without having written anything. As I walked, I wondered how Abby was making out and whether my aging life would allow me a final good story.

8

Abby came home after having worked eight and a half hours in emergency, which had received a flurry of patients from major traffic, construction and industrial accidents. I had prepared pasta and a salad before she arrived and set the table while she showered. I was keenly aware that what I was dealing with and struggling over was fiction. The absurdity of talking to her about my problems of character, dialogue, plot and images while all day she helped people facing life and death issues was a constant reality check. We didn't talk much during the meal. She went to the bedroom and put her head down on the pillow. I stood in the doorway looking at her, thinking of a way to apologize for my insensitive comment earlier without making a fool of myself. Then she saved me as she had so often done. She held out her hand and asked me to lie beside her. She turned and snuggled into me. I wanted to say I'm sorry again for the thoughtless remark, but before I could, she said, "Tell me about your day, my love. Tell me something good happened." I held her close and kissed her cheek. How could I not love her? "I had a good day, Abby. It got even better when I came home."

We cuddled close after reading for a while. Abby needed the distraction of a good plot-driven story and the warmth of a good hug. After half an hour, she put the book down. "Give me a hug, Jacob; I'm tired. I'm going to sleep." I never could hold her enough.

The next morning after breakfast, while I cleaned up, she got herself ready and left, fully prepared for the surprises the day would hold for her. I put my pen and ink in my satchel along with a *Rhodia* notepad and loose sheets of notes I had made at 3 in the morning. I was still having difficulty sleeping and often rose in the middle of the night to work.

It was another bright, sunny day with a light, warm breeze wandering carelessly through the downtown streets. Before going in the café, I stood on the sidewalk and let the sun play on my face. I needed the warmth. Since my heart surgery, I never let a day go by without being grateful to be alive. I opened the door and walked in. The place was empty. I took my seat at the table by the window and ordered a decaf Americano. When the young waitress returned, she laid the cup on the table then pulled back the curtain of the window, allowing the sunlight to pour in and cover me. I took out my notes and fountain pen, a black Pilot 912 with a soft-medium nib filled with *Iroshizuku Kon-peki* ink and continued writing where I had left off last night. A few people entered the café; then half an hour later, Lorne entered and went to his usual table. He pulled out his notebooks and pens and looked over the crowd. He smiled and came over. "Do you mind if I sit and chat before getting down to work?"

"Not at all," I told him. He went to get a couple of cups of espresso. Looking back, he said, "Decaf, right?" I nodded. It was a two-cup morning.

As we conversed, I learned that he too was a retired professor of literature. "I did 35 mostly happy years, including six as department head here at the university." We shared stories and finally discussed what we were working on.

I told him I had outlined a story about Baruch Spinoza and Uriel da Costa then put it aside. "I'm not ready for it yet. Then the other day out of the blue I began humming Psalm 133, *Hine ma tov u'ma na-im/Shevet achim gam ya-chad*. Do you know it?"

"I do as a matter of fact even though I haven't been to synagogue for years."

"Behold, how good and how pleasant it is for brothers also to dwell together in unity. It's a nice sentiment; however, we should understand it as meaning 'for everyone to dwell together in unity'. When has that ever happened?"

"You are cynical. Must be all the coffee you're drinking."

"Then I started thinking of how I could turn it into a murder mystery and how I could bring Odysseus into it, but not returning from Troy, but rather deciding to leave Ithaka to fight in the Trojan War in order to avoid someone's wrath and revenge on the island."

"I like that. He went to Troy to save his ass."

"It interests me. I won't know until I begin if I can go anywhere with it. You can tell very quickly if it merits the effort and whether you can bring it off. It might end up as just another story idea that remains in the notebook."

"We're never certain, are we? We write a great paragraph then the next day we rethink it because of something we've found that wants to enter the world of the story. So we rework everything. I'm not the kind of writer who spends time planning an elaborate architecture of a story. I prefer the bricolage method, constructing or creating from a diverse range of available ideas and things. It's the excitement of the moment as words and images provoke in certain directions. Every time I sit at my desk or that table over there, a myriad of things come into focus that may have nothing to do with the plot or characters, but I try to work them at the moment because they might suggest certain ways to advance. It might not work out one time, but it might the next."

He sipped the *crema* from the top of his coffee. "Sorry for going on. I'd like to hear more about your novel."

"Bricolage, yes. After teaching literature for so many years, I've been liberated from the dictates of the finely crafted novel publishers insist on, the kind that makes the curricula or the bestseller lists."

"You're deflecting, Jacob. Don't you want to talk about your present work?"

"Yes, I'm deflecting, and no, I don't want to discuss the manuscript under my elbows.

"Sometimes I'm convinced that there's more than a little envy in the attitude. I mean, wouldn't we all like to have a major publisher take one of our stories?"

"For sure. But at my age, I have nothing to prove. I've published books. Now I'm free to explore. That's what's important to me."

As we conversed, Lorne continued to rub a dark spot next to his left sideburn. I asked him if he was all right and pointed to the side of his face. "Oh, that. My dermatologist found some precancerous cells and zapped them with liquid nitrogen. The skin is still a little sensitive." He saw the expression on my face. "No, I'm all right. Really. They're gone. When you reach a certain age, every medical issue is a crisis in waiting."

We finished our coffee and continued talking about our lives. "Well, Jacob, I'd better get to work. When you're ready, I'd like to hear about your story."

"I'll send you a signed copy when it's out."

"Thank you. Next time, I'll tell you about intrigue among the Jews of Armenia. Perhaps by then I'll have found an answer to how god sacrificed his stiff-necked people in the Shoah and the Armenians in the 1915 genocide."

On the way home, I mused that we were both more than a little obscure in our subject matter. There's no end to ideas one can explore, yet even today with desktop publishing and print on demand, publishers, online media and the critical mafia still run the show. I won't bring this bitterness home to Abby.

9

In a course on exile and literature I taught during my last ten years at the university, much of the critical debates as well as memoirs left by writers themselves revolved around the following semantic cluster: exiles, emigrés, refugees, expatriates, nomads and cosmopolitans. The words that most closely defined what our family lived through were exiles and refugees. My parents faced political banishment as the Nazis removed any notion of choice; if you were a Jew, you were marked for death. My family left their home yet again, this time after living 450 years in Salonica. The first time, of course, happened in 1492 after the royal edicts produced The Tribunal of the Holy Office of the Inquisition, *El Tribunal del Santo Oficio de la Inquisición*, which was designed to regulate the faith of newly converted Catholics and was intensified after the royal decrees issued in 1492 and 1502 ordering Jews and Muslims to convert to Catholicism or leave Spain. It is an ironic shifting of numbers that sealed the fate for my parents and other Jews: 1492 was the year of the expulsion of Jews from Spain and 1942 was the year the Nazis began rounding up Jews in Salonica first for slave labour then later to be sent to Auschwitz. In Spain our fate was the following, become a *converso*, convert, or die; then 450 years later it was stay in Salonica and die. Choose exile and you might survive as a refugee. In both cases it was political banishment. My mother and father survived and lived with geographical and physical displacement and spiritual estrangement. Being a Jew meant you constantly lived with the melancholy tension of separation from your origins. In their forced departures, they became outsiders once again, wandering Jews, displaced, restless, uprooted, the universal strangers. It was only much later that my parents were able to transform the physical displacement of exile into possibilities of interior experience that saved them. It took a long time, however. Every night I could hear my parents whisper so they wouldn't wake me, wondering how they were going to live. Through her tears, my mother took in clothes to be repaired. My father could only find part-time work that diminished his sense of worth. Yet he continued to write and sell articles and stories to the refugee press in the country until he won a position at New York University that changed all of our lives.

As refugees, they were literally homeless; as Jewish refugees, they had an acute sense of metaphorical homelessness that always put into question home and nationhood, home and culture. I was born in New York, but I did live their dislocation until I grew up and claimed my place in the city. Having had such a long history in Salonica made the rupture and loss of family and friends even more complete. Transplanted in New York, my parents assimilated as much as they needed to and held on to their past as much as they could. In the end, they regained their lives.

Growing up, there were always stories of Tía Ruth or Tío Salomón, the amazing picnics, sailing excursions on the Aegean, and always how they all disappeared. All they could take were their memories. As I grew older and gained experience, my stories and references were displaced by those of my parents. Their exile and marginalization always forced them to consider themselves in diaspora and that home was elsewhere. For a time, it took over my life. One Sunday when other Jews from Salonica gathered at our place, I sat and listened to their stories, the jokes, the explosions of laughter when a certain person or an event was recalled. That was the moment when I realized that no matter how much I loved my parents for what they had accomplished given the adversity they had lived through, I didn't share that part of their identity. The most I could do was write about the absence of these memories and the presence of that absence. I quickly came to realize that this wasn't very satisfying. The best way to honour my parents, I felt, was to be honest about who I was becoming. I was disconnected from their memories even though I felt their emotional resonance. They sought connections to what only could be retrieved in memory. My father was able to use this loss to create in his books what he could never recover; he imagined what he could not remember and mourned the irreversible loss.

Understanding this, I was able to write about it from outside experience, close but nevertheless without the lived, first-hand references and experiences. This was my weakness, perhaps, being too close yet unable or unwilling to live their lives with them and their past, sing their songs. This is why about 15 years ago I chose to study the life of Uriel da Costa, born in 1584, a Jewish-Portuguese converso, from Oporto who had converted to Catholicism, and whose life the Inquisition subsequently twisted into a sad fate after he returned to Judaism in Amsterdam. I was searching for a parallel to what my parents lived through 325 years later in 1942-43. What had exile, being a refugee, and living in diaspora done to their lives? It forced me to consider the journey I had taken as I struck out on my own. More importantly, what does it mean for me at this stage in my life? Does da Costa's sorrowful life offer an exemplum when one is uprooted and pursued? I hoped it didn't, but what happened to him was a cautionary tale.

Uriel da Costa was born into a *converso* family from Oporto, Portugal, in 1584. His father was a devout Christian who raised his son to be a pious Catholic. Da Costa studied law, but before long, certain character traits became clear that would have an effect on his later life: he hated to suffer attacks and disliked arrogant people who put others down.

Like most at that time, he feared eternal damnation and kept to all the doctrines; however, the more he read the gospels the more he became overwhelmed with grief. He believed confession was not a way out and thought that only following the rules would lead to salvation.

He became unsatisfied with Christianity, and upon reading the Torah, he believed that everything was revealed by God himself. He then decided to leave Portugal with his mother and brothers for Amsterdam in order to practice Judaism freely, or so he thought. In his new city, he immediately got circumcised and converted.

Before long, he ran into difficulty with the local customs which he found different from the laws of Moses and had run-ins with the rabbis. He called them obstinate and perverse. The rabbis told him that if he didn't follow their teaching, they would exclude him from their synagogue. Da Costa refused to recant and as a result, was excommunicated. Even his brothers rejected him and refused to acknowledge him on the street.

The rabbis asked Menasseh Ben Israel, a famous Portuguese rabbi, kabbalist, writer, and founder of the first Hebrew printing press in Amsterdam in 1626, to write a treatise against da Costa's ideas. Ben Israel wrote *Of the*

Immortality of the Soul, in which da Costa is accused of defending Epicurean principles and denying the soul.

Not content with excommunicating him, the rabbis set the children against da Costa, insulting him, spitting at him, abusing him, crying out, "There goes a heretic; there goes an Apostate." Often, they assembled at his front door and threw stones at his windows.

Da Costa wrote a treatise, *Eleven Theses Against the Tradition*, countering Ben Israel's book. Unable to countenance his behaviour, the community decided to go to the public magistrate to lay charges against him that his book attempted to disprove the immortality of the soul with a view to subvert, not only the Jewish, but Christian religions. Da Costa was sent to prison for 10 days and fined 300 florins and forfeited his new book. In time, da Costa realized that it would be easier for him to accept the rabbis and to conform. He formally recanted and accepted the articles imposed on him. Nevertheless, his problems with the Jewish community continued; even his family turned on him. If he did not submit to the rabbis, he was to be excommunicated again. The Sanhedrin, an assembly of rabbis appointed to sit as a tribunal, considered charges questioning if he really was a Jew. Ever recalcitrant, da Costa refused and was again excommunicated. He was spit upon in the street and was completely rejected and isolated. Unable to tolerate this, he accepted the terms of the tribunal, "I depend upon your mercy and am ready to undergo whatsoever you are pleased to impose on me." His sentence called for him to make a public recantation, suffer a whipping, followed by him prostrating himself at the door of the synagogue so that all in the community can walk over him. At the end of his ordeal, the rabbi said, "Now the gate of heaven barred to you is open." Then he was to fast for a number of days.

Da Costa wrote his autobiography, *Exemplar Humanae Vitae* in 1640. He was unable to forgive his cousin who had turned on him and plotted to kill him and himself. Then one day as he saw his cousin approach, he grabbed a pistol and pulled the trigger, but it misfired. He pulled out another and turned in on himself and fired. He died an agonizing death.

It is an unbelievable story, yet perhaps it is but one extreme example of what some conversos had to go through when they returned to Judaism in a new country. Da Costa was an unfortunate hero battling religious intolerance. He believed that religion was a disruptive element against natural law as well as a source of hatred and superstition. He proposed a faith based on natural law and reason and can be considered a precursor and perhaps even an inspiration to Baruch Spinoza, who was eight when da Costa died.

As I recall the time when I studied the life of da Costa, I see now as I did then that his story forces each of us to ask how far one is willing to go and how much one is willing to give up for what one believes in the fight to free oneself from superstition. His story is an example of what can happen when freedom of thought and freedom of worship are compromised.

What interested me as the son of a Jewish family that had suffered two diasporas is that da Costa's life is indicative of the problems many Marranos dealt with when they arrived in an organized Jewish community in a new country. In confronting an organized rabbinic community, he had difficulty dealing with the established rituals and doctrines of orthodox rabbinical Judaism such as the oral law. In the end, da Costa was a lonely intellectual, ill at ease with traditional Jewish ways and yet very consistent in his fight against intolerance. Regaining one's life and a sense of normalcy after all had been taken away generations earlier can be an impossible pursuit. In time, embracing the rupture can bring forth something new, vibrant and viable. My father had no choice but to accept the loss, but through his creativity, he was able to reimagine his life and bring to his writing a new perspective on the past, the object of his research and writing.

10

No, I'm not da Costa although I have felt alienated from the community my parents belonged to and longed for in the diaspora. However, since my retirement, I have tried to find something to attach myself to. When I left the university, a major part of my life came to an end. I never looked for a way back. In any case, none was possible. I needed to move on and so have found myself in Toronto, damaged. By some miracle, Devorah, my former wife, came to my rescue. It was more than I deserved. She helped restore my health and introduced me to Abby, whom I love deeply. If I were smart, I would leave it at that. What more do I need for a peaceful life? But I am driven. I can't be content with things as they are. Because of this, I feel a certain sympathy for da Costa despite his willful tendency to create problems for himself. Yet in his mind, he acted out of the conviction that he was right. I can't say that I have a distinct set of guiding principles as my parents had. Now at this stage of my life, I find myself floating through life, anxious and restless.

For some time now, I've been struggling with this novel I've been writing. My daily effort has become confused with recovery from my heart surgery, Abby going off to the hospital every day and now my meeting Lorne and Jake. Abby and I don't see each other as much as we use to. I miss her, but I don't want to become overly possessive of her. It just underlines the fact that I'm older than she is, perhaps too much older. My professional life has ended while hers continues. I'm comfortable in her love as I think she is in mine. I guess I've become more needy lately. On top of this, I've been thinking of my parents a lot recently. I'm not able to put any of this aside and focus on the book. My mind is awash with many disparate elements I'm unable to contain and compartmentalize safely. At times it feels as if there's a whirlpool spinning and spinning, dragging everything down into the abyss.

I wanted to write some more this evening before Abby returned from a late shift, but I kept wondering about a meeting tomorrow with Lorne and Jake we had arranged yesterday at the café. I like them and enjoy sharing literary talk. But I've never had any close friends with whom I've shared my personal life and my writing apart from Devorah and Abby. I've always worked alone. There are benefits to this, but there are also downsides. Since I met Abby, my life has improved so much, and I hope she feels the same. It must be my age that makes me feel so uncertain about things. There's a restless anxiety about everything. Recently, I've had to search for words, something I never had to do before. I second guess myself and look for the easy way out in discussions when I know better having been a professor for so long. It's disconcerting. I know that at my age it likely will not improve, the opposite in fact. I have to prepare for this. Writing this book is a way for me to know that I'm still capable of sustained thought, and can develop themes and characters, images.

This morning I heard a thud at the living room window. I went to see what it was and found a wounded starling lying on the floor of the balcony, unable to spread one of its wings. It just lay there making a pitiful, unsuccessful effort to lift off. It clawed at the concrete and tried to move its wings but was only able to move in a circle. I didn't know what to do. The vet I called told me there was nothing I could do if its wing was broken. "Can you bring it in?" he asked. I picked it up carefully. It was as light as air. As I placed it in a paper bag, it made hurt sounds. When I got to the vet's 40 minutes later, he opened the bag and found it lying at the bottom dead.

11

Lorne, Jake, and I had decided to meet at 8:30 that evening to talk about the progress of our stories. Now that Abby was working nights, I was able to work late. I wasn't sleeping well anyway. When she was home, I wanted to give her all my attention. It had been getting dark earlier recently as the world was turning on its axis. Tonight, the air was chilly and was a warning of what would soon be coming. When I arrived at the café, I found Jake sitting at our usual table, staring out the window. When I greeted him, he quickly looked at me and nodded then continued looking around outside.

"What's going on, Jake?" I asked. His eyes darted from the people sitting around us to what was happening outside the café.

"Did you see a tall, thin guy, dark hair, hanging around outside the café?"

"Lots of guys fit that description, why?"

"That's Al, you know, the guy who kidnapped me. He saw me a week ago. I can't shake him." Beads of sweat had formed on his upper lip. "Every time I go out, he's there."

"What does he want?"

"What the hell do you think? I killed his brother. He wants to kill me. The last time I saw him, he pointed his fingers like a gun at me. He won't rest until he gets me."

Every time someone entered the café, he jerked around to see who it was. Even the sound of a chair being pulled out frightened him. "Lorne will be here soon. Al won't touch you if he sees the three of us."

"And if he gets me alone? You don't know what he's capable of."

"How did he find you?"

"Purely by chance. He saw me coming out of my agent's office on Bay Street near College. The moment I saw him, I knew it was him, that bastard. Before I could turn the other way, he saw me. He gave me that cold look, the same way he did when he chained me to a pipe in his warehouse. He followed me. Luckily, I lost him in the subway at Yonge Street. He won't give up. He's going to kill me."

"Why can't you go to the police?"

"I'd have to tell them I killed his brother and the Swede. How do you think that would work out for me?"

"But they had kidnapped you. Isn't that self defence, justifiable homicide?"

"A good lawyer could turn it against me. Who knows what I would get?"

Just then Lorne came in. The sound of the door closing caused Jake to shudder. He came over and sat at the table. "Why so serious?"

I told him, "The guy who kidnapped Jake a few years back is stalking him. He could be anywhere near here."

"You're kidding. Okay, let's think this through. First of all, let's get out of here. You're going to have to change your routines, Jake."

"You're plotting this like a novel," Jake told him.

"Just trying to help."

"Listen, I'll go out first," I said, "then Lorne then Jake. Agreed?"

Jake pulled out his keys. "My car's just around the corner."

"We've got your back, Jake."

Jake thanked us and waited behind as we exited. Lorne and I stopped in front of the door to the café. We talked and looked around; then Lorne went in and told Jake it was okay to come out. For a moment I felt we were in a gangster film, making sure the coast was clear to avoid a hit before the boss came out, except we were writers. I wasn't certain we could write our way out of this. The moment Jake came out we followed him to his car, got in and took off.

We drove around in silence for a while taking side streets. "I'm going to show you where this started," Jake said. We drove for another 25 minutes then pulled over and parked on Manor Road. "This is where Hannah and I lived. I often park here and watch her through her window. She lives here with the detective thief who was on my case. He didn't solve a thing and stole my wife. According to everyone at the time, I had just disappeared. What else could Hannah do? From everything I saw through the window, how could I have gone back to her?"

We sat back and settled into a series of rambling conversations about our novels and our lives, how fickle life can be. Every now and then Jake would say, "Look, there she is," and we'd all look over to see Hannah and her husband. I fell asleep for a while then was startled awake by loud banging on the driver's side window.

"Open the door you son-of-a-bitch!" somebody yelled. "Open up! You're not getting away this time!"

"It's Al!" Jake yelled and fumbled trying to start the car.

I was sitting in the back behind Jake and opened my door with force that caught Al unprepared and threw him backwards off balance causing him to fall hard onto a fire hydrant. He cracked the side of his head with a bone crunching smack and fell to the ground in a heap. His legs quivered a few times; then he went still. We all got out and checked him. "Is he breathing?" Lorne asked. We rolled him over and checked for a pulse but couldn't find one. Jake listened for a breath.

"In the movies they always check for a breath with a mirror."

"Well, sorry," Lorne said. "I left my purse at home."

"He's dead. He's dead." I looked at the others. "Now what are we going to do? We can't leave him here."

"I have an idea," Jake said, "but we have to act quickly. Help me lift him."

"I can't lift anything after my bypass surgery," I said.

Lorne and Jake lifted Al's lifeless body onto the back seat and folded him down so no one could see him. I got in next to Al. Lorne climbed in the front next to Jake. As we pulled away, I looked over to Hannah's house and saw her silhouette looking at us through her front window.

"What have we done?"

"Come on, Jacob, he was going to kill Jake."

"One less problem," Jake said coldly. "One less thing to worry about in this world."

As Jake headed toward the eastbound lanes of the 401, the refrain kept playing in my mind. "Is it, is it really?"

When I looked back out the rear window as we were pulling away, I saw Hannah's husband run out of the house and down the driveway towards where we were parked. He's a detective, I thought. What could he have seen?

12

"Slow down, Jake, for God's sake," I said with more than a little anger. "We don't want to get pulled over." Jake swerved around a slower car, throwing Al onto me. He bounced off my shoulder and fell back. His head hit the arm rest on door and turned back over towards me. I found myself starring at his beady eyes and dilated pupils. They were like a lizard's when it's about to strike. It was creepy. I was angry and told Lorne to make sure Jake sticks to the speed limit. Jake was hearing none of it. He had the needle of the speedometer stuck at 120 as he blew past Pickering, Ajax, and Oshawa. We saw flashing red lights on the shoulder up ahead where a police cruiser had pulled over a group of teenagers crammed into a green pickup truck. Only then did Jake slow down until we were past them. The sign indicating Bowmanville was a blur as was the one indicating Newcastle. Suddenly he hit the brakes and steered onto the off ramp at Port Hope. Just great, I thought, Port Hope. Not for Al and maybe not for us. He guided his car onto Rose Glen Road then turned left onto Ontario Street. There was moisture in the air that gave the light coming from the streetlamps an eerie, blurry glow. Then past the Tim Horton's whose parking lot was jammed full then past Shoppers Simply Pharmacy right onto Highway 2 and a quick left again and south onto the continuation of John Street. In the dark I hardly had time to read the street signs as Jake wheeled around corners and raced down roads. Hayward Street and more sharp turns throwing Al onto me at every corner until Jake brought the car to a gravely sliding stop in the parking lot of West Beach. Bloody Port Hope Beach. It sounded like a resort just this side of paradise.

"How the hell do you know this place?" Lorne asked.

"As a teenager we use to make midnight runs to all the small towns along the lake outside Toronto. It was something to do. We'd stop for burgers and fries along the way." He saw Lorne and me give each other a look. "I know. It was the beginning of my misspent life." Neither Lorne nor I were about to disagree.

Jake got out of the car and looked around. "There's no one around. Let's pull him out of the car and take him down to the lake."

"We should stay out of the pools of lights. They're all over the beach," Lorne said.

I didn't want any part of this. I had told them that we had to take Al to the hospital and that if we didn't, we risked getting into a lot of trouble. "Sure," Jake said. "You can tell the police it was you who knocked him into the fire hydrant and that he didn't wake up. That it was you who killed him."

"We can't do this. It's not decent," I said.

"You saw how violent he was. He wasn't decent. He ruined my life, my marriage. No. I want rid of him."

At that moment, it confirmed to me once again that I had become a moral coward. For a moment I saw myself in jail, hoping a large crowd would show up at my execution to hurl insults as the guillotine fell on my neck, but I was no Meursault. Lorne and Jake grabbed Al from the back seat and pulled him onto the beach that was a random collection of sticks, stones, and sand that made it difficult to walk and carry the weight. "I'll lug the guts," Lorne chuckled. "This is hardly a Shakespearean moment," I said. "Give us a hand then," Lorne whispered and raised Al's body to his shoulders as if we were carrying him to a Viking funeral boat. "Let's do this and get out of here."

I held up one of Al's legs and went down to the water's edge with them. As if to cooperate, the full moon momentarily slipped behind a bank of dark clouds as Jake stepped into the lake and pulled Al out into the water. Just as quickly, the light of the treacherous moon suddenly reappeared. Jake stumbled and fell back into the water. "He moved! I think he moved! The bugger's not dead. How the...."

"Let's take him to the local hospital," I said, but before I finished, Jake shoved me back, causing me to trip over Al's legs. I landed on my back on a bunch of large stones at the water's edge. When I got up, Jake had already pushed Al's face under water and held it there for some time. He stood up and looked at us. "Okay," he said under his breath. He grabbed Al's body and pulled him out into deeper water and finally let the body float out into the lake, "That's done it," he said, "Let's get the hell out of here."

We piled back into the car and before long got back onto the westbound 401. "No speeding, Jake," Lorne said.

"Not a problem anymore. Not a problem."

I didn't believe it.

13

When I got home sometime after 3 am, I put my clothes in the laundry hamper and took a shower. I needed to sleep but was too wired. I kept seeing the car door fly open, knocking Al backwards onto the large iron valve protruding from the top of the fire hydrant and the sickening crack as his head fell onto it with force. We should have taken him to an emergency room, but we let ourselves be carried away on the angry wave of Jake's revenge. Lorne and I should have been firmer. How long will it be before the trail leads back to us? How far have I strayed? I just wanted a peaceful retirement and had heart surgery; I just wanted to finish one last book and ended up killing someone I don't even know, who had done me no harm. I had found Abby and fallen in love. She rescued me from myself and gave me hope for a better life at my age, good enough at least, something close to what I wanted. She helps me deal with the constant ill-at-ease, this restlessness that plagues me. Every day I set goals for myself no matter how small or ambitious they might be. Usually, they include a walk after breakfast then at least two hours writing before lunch. For the past months I had been going to Waterman's Café where I met Lorne and Jake. What kept me returning there? Jake was a constant ball of anger who will never finish his novel unless he wants to turn it into one of self-recrimination, a memoir of revenge and murder. Hopefully he would change the names to protect the guilty. On the way back to the city, Lorne took out his pen and notebook and made notes for the duration of the trip. I'll bet he's at work right now turning it all into a lurid, psychological crime story. Two guilt-ridden Jews out to help a fellow writer, another Jew, rescue his life from the maniac who stole it. We did it without pen and ink; we used Al's blood instead. I can still see Jake on top of Al holding his head under water. Truthfully, I didn't see air bubbles coming from Al's nose or mouth. Maybe he was already dead. That doesn't absolve me of anything. My back is so sore from landing on the stones at the water's edge, thanks to Jake. Every time I move, the pain is a reminder of my guilt.

I heard Abby open the front door. I looked at the alarm clock: 4:30. I couldn't face her, not yet. I had to camouflage everything: I worked at the café then came back to put it on the computer to edit. I watched a little tv then went to bed around midnight. I had a very uneventful night. I'll add that some pain came up in my right hip. I think it might be sciatica. She'll tell me to check it out tomorrow. I will. I'll bring in the constant metaphysical discomfort: my age, the writing, the need to complete projects to leave at least a written record to confirm that I was here if only for a while. I'm not vain enough to believe it might be a legacy. My father, on the other hand, believed that everything he did and wrote after the Holocaust was important because of the precariousness of their lives. He believed their survival made them accountable. In my case, the students, academic essays, poems and plays, a book of fiction and this novel I'm trying to complete doesn't seem to count for much. Nevertheless, I am compelled to finish it for my father and mother. There must be something to show I was here, that we were here. I would add my voice to my father's and mother's. I can't help but thinking that in the end, who's looking anyway? It's all vanity, a murderer's pride.

After her shower, Abby climbed into bed and kissed me. I feigned sleep. She wrapped her arms around me and whispered, "I love you," as she did every night and lay her head on my shoulder. I didn't deserve her love. Would she still say I love you if she knew I was a killer?

I closed my eyes tighter and fell into the rhythm of Abby's breathing until I was no longer aware of breathing. I dreamt of my Mother and Father. What would they say of what I had become? I didn't do it on purpose, *Madre. Fue un accidente, Padre.* For a moment I became their young son looking for absolution again.

14

It's been a week since the "event." I've tried to be my usual self when Abby and I are together, but I know she suspects something is bothering me. She's asked me several times if everything is okay. "You look and sound off, tentative, Jacob." I tell her that the novel is weighing heavily on my mind. "I want to finish it soon in case I'm no longer able to." She tells me my health is fine. "Whatever is happening is going on in your mind, my love." I tell her I'm all right. "It's just a difficult passage I have to get through." She wonders why I don't take a break, leave it for a while. "You'll come back to it with fresh eyes, new ideas." She's not wrong, of course except that what's disturbing me is not so easy to overcome. While I'm agonizing, I'll bet Lorne is filling pages. He thrives on this sort of thing. When Jake jumped on Al and held his head underwater, Lorne just stood there, watching, noting the position of Jake's hands, observing Al's face distorted by the ripples and the moon's refraction in the water. Even on the way back into the city, he continued to make notes. It was as if the whole thing was made for him, set up for him to observe. I'm not sure he feels any remorse.

As for me, I'm sailing through the rough waters of my fears and the stormy seas of my desires. I know I'll never find the peace and calm of a resolution. I had hoped for slightly more from my retirement. I've now become unhopeful and stiff. I've lost the ability to bend to circumstances then bounce back.

Like Odysseus, lashed to the mast, I refuse to be wrecked on the illusion that life is fair or just. There is no such previous world I long for. To continue the analogy that seems to be apt as I'm scratching this down in my notepad, I'll stay with the ship, anchored to the present and wrestle as my Hebrew namesake did with the treachery and complexity of life. There are moments when the need to return home is overlaid or confused with the promise of something new, a new life, an opportunity to break away from fate. As if one can sidestep whatever impediments life flings at us. Alas, I feel there is no sense that virtue might be compensated or that weakness could be shielded. Confronted by the choices life forces us to consider, we navigate between the whirlpool and the rocks. Homer says, there is nothing sweeter to a man than his own country. That's what my parents believed. But which one: the one in Spain, Salonica, America, or going back to the beginning, Israel? To these I have to add Canada. There is nothing sweeter than my own country. I wish I could believe this. In truth, however, nothing is more unsettled and disquieting than a man's own country regardless that it is the site where desire and sweetness are the most intense.

Abby is my island. Our companionship is our understanding of the world we share. Every night she wraps her arms around me and kisses me. Regardless of what she has seen in the emergency room, she always tells me before we close our eyes that tomorrow is another day to live and to navigate clear of the rocky shore. I hold her tight and cannot bring myself to tell her about Port Hope.

In my head I hear the waves breaking over the jagged shore. I put my arms around Abby and hold tight.

15

Several weeks have passed since we put Al in the lake. I saw a brief news report of a body being found on the beach at Port Hope. Foul play is suspected. Then nothing. A week after that on the six-o'clock news, a connection was found between the deceased and a series of robberies in the east end of Toronto. Gang connections were mentioned followed by the speculation that the hit was likely a settling of accounts. And that was it. No other news followed. The whole thing drifted away in the vast ocean of old news items: a woman was struck and killed crossing Eglinton Avenue, a cat was rescued by firemen in Rosedale, and the American president berates Canada over perceived trade imbalances. I felt somewhat relieved. But not absolved. Every night, I went to bed expecting to be wakened by a loud knock at the door.

Six months have flown by. I have slipped back into my old routine as if nothing had ever happened. I have not spoken to Lorne or Jake since, although Lorne sent me a copy of his latest book, a crime thriller set by a lake in small town Ontario, published by Gallows Press. This was a new genre for him, but then he liked experimenting and expanding his repertoire. As I read through it, it felt a little too familiar for comfort, even though the characters and action were not similar, they were close enough to trigger my guilty conscience. In his dedication written in red fountain pen ink, he had written, "Thanks for the material. I'm looking forward to reading your version." I wrote a short note of congratulations in my favourite blue ink,

Pilot's *Iroshizuku kon-peki*. I knew he would continue to turn every found scrap into a narrative and using the bricolage method, weave it into a larger literary narrative that would become his next book. I wished him good luck and hinted that we shouldn't contact each other for some time. I haven't heard from Jake, but I'll wager he regularly parks in front of Hannah's house on Manor Road, sitting in silence, boiling at how Al and his gang ruined his life. No revenge will ever make that right. Writing his novel will not heal the damage.

I like to think that I've almost finished my novel; however, every time I put down my pen, a new idea sparks a few more pages. I'm going to continue writing until I'm finished; that is, the story.

Three weeks ago, Abby decided to retire and gave her notice. Now we have a lot of free time for ourselves. Last night we talked about travelling. She suggested we go to Salonica then on to Israel. "It would be like going home, Jacob," she said. I've been thinking about this, and my mood vacillates between excitement at the possibility and fear.

16

So many self-recriminations after all these years. At times I feel as if I am Lucius Sergius Catilina whom Cicero denounced in the Roman Senate in 63 BCE for plotting to overthrow the government. I am at a standstill in my 73'rd year. Any notion of me overthrowing anything is laughable. In his first speech, Cicero accused Catilina, *Quo usque tandem abutere, Catilina, patientia nostra? Quam diu etiam furor iste tuus nos eludet?* I can still hear Professor Orr in the Classics seminar I took in third year at Harvard, asking me to translate this in front of the class. "When, O Catiline, do you mean to cease abusing our patience? How long is that madness of yours still to mock us?" Today, I would say, "When O Jacob…."

Then bouts of writer's block interspersed with moments of madness and nightmares of murder. One then the other, back and forth, writer's block, lunacy, murder. Waiting for the knock at the door.

Some days I think I've finished the story. On several occasions I've written in blue *Kon-Peki* ink in my Pilot 912 fountain pen at the bottom of what I had hoped was the final page, The End. Then I hear the echo, how long is that madness of yours still to mock us? Recently, I put the manuscript away and have begun learning Hebrew as a way to distract my mind. When you're detached from everything but the story you're living which you believe will give you a reprieve, an answer, you're delusional.

Questions remain, where am I going? Where's home? The only answer I've found is that I don't know where I'm going and likely never will. As for home, it's where I'm comfortable and safe, and that is in Abby's arms.

17

This morning, a padded mailing envelope containing the preface of Jake Calman's new novel, *After Hannah*, arrived in the mail. I was apprehensive. What was he going to reveal? It was accompanied by a short note.

Jacob,

I hope you're well and that the ink from your fountain pen flows abundantly. I haven't seen you at the café recently, but then I don't go as often as I use to. I've been working hard to finish *After Hannah*. I've enclosed a draft of the preface for your interest and comments. No doubt the title of the *fictional* preface, "West Beach," will arouse your curiosity. I think I've been able to turn what happened to me into a fictional narrative using the memoir, murder mystery and detective story genres. As if masking the real creates enough distance from what I'm still dealing with. But then since Port Hope, the three of us are living with our own secrets.

I had a long talk with Ari Grimm last week. He has agreed to put my book on his publishing list for fiction next year. It's enough to keep me focused and away from bad memories and harmful habits.

Hannah and Jon are still living together. I can't get over it. I still park in front of our house and watch them. It's a curse I'm living with. I'll have a new book, but I'll never have Hannah again.

I'd love to meet you and Lorne for coffee at the café, but I think it's wise not to for some time.

WEST BEACH (where things end and begin)

I've been going to the Waterman Bookstore Café for some time now, trying to write myself back to some level of normalcy. Two years ago, I was kidnapped for seven months by three low-level gangsters, extortionists. I was working at *Bottoms Up*, a bar on Bayview Avenue in quiet Leaside. I was alone on the night shift when a large guy started punching a small, skinny bloke sitting at the same table. I had to step in to protect the bar. I'm tall and in good shape and took care of the guy, Dan his name was. He picked himself up and as he was limping towards the door, he swore payback. After closing, I walked back to our home on Manor Road and stopped on the walk as I always did to look at my wife Hannah framed in the front window. I remember smiling as I was looking forward to holding her in my arms again when a loud thud on the back of my head put me out. When I woke, I was bouncing around on the back seat of a car beside Dan, who was punching me in the ribs. I heard him and his two buddies talking over what they should do with me. Two of the three said that they should get rid of me, throw me over the Scarborough Bluffs. Then the driver, Al, the leader, said they should think it through a little further. I wasn't worth doing life for. Their corporate decision was to take me out with them on their nightly collections until they felt they could trust me to join their crew. This way they would always have something over me. This would be my punishment. They taught me the ropes of their business which involved lending money to needy people who couldn't get financing from anywhere else. Then they would aggressively collect every month. If someone didn't pay, the boys would take something that belonged to the client. If that didn't encourage a payment, Dan would pay the person a visit. This usually proved successful. It wasn't hard to catch on to what they were about. They were thieves preying on the vulnerable. Before long, I became a visible member of their crew, a criminal. I couldn't turn them in without implicating myself as their accomplice. They made it very clear that If I ran away or went to the police, they would kill Hannah. What choice did I have? The more I went out collecting with them, the more I took perverse pleasure in the work. I encouraged the victims to pay something to avoid violence and often served as an intermediary between them and the boys. It was distracting and put the boys at ease to see me working with their victims. I admit that occasionally I had to strong arm a few, but I always whispered an apology to them before I did. To rub salt in my wounds, the boys often drove and parked in front of my home and relished showing me how the detective on my missing persons case, Jon, they told me, had become a little too friendly with Hannah and how she was responding to his advances. There had been no word from me, no clues as to my whereabouts for months. In everyone's mind, I had disappeared, and this allowed detective Jon the freedom to replace me. Apparently, Hannah had come to accept this. As time passed, I couldn't take it anymore. I had written a memoir of my captivity and had hidden it in a plastic bag in the toilet tank in the warehouse where I was held. Not only had I lost my life, but I was being erased and supplanted. My wife was abandoning me for this detective who was searching for me. I tried rationalizing it. What could she do after all? Maybe I was dead or had run away with another woman. Was it fair for her to wait and put her life on hold?

Finally, the opportunity came for me to escape. Dan and I had just completed a collection on Lawrence Avenue East and returned to their warehouse on Eastern Avenue where every night they chained me to a thick metal pipe. So much for trust. When Dan tried to tie my hands, I kicked him in the scrotum, twice, then electrocuted him. I had a lot of pent up anger eating away at me. I wrapped him up and put him in the back seat of the car and drove to the bluffs and threw him over. He tumbled and rolled down over the rocks then splashed into the lake. Bye-bye, Dan. You ruined my life. A little later, I found myself alone with Soren, whom I called the philosopher of the gang. Al was out seeing his girlfriend, Jocasta McEwan, a fiery Scot, mixed-martial arts fighter who had won seven of her last ten fights. The few times I saw her, her face was bruised and puffy. She always stood next to Al, brooding. One time, she opened her bag and showed me the dagger she always kept with her, ma dirk, she called it. She smiled revealing that one of her canine teeth was missing. I wouldn't want to be on her bad side. Soren's back was turned as he was arranging his collection of Kierkegaard on the shelf. I wasn't going to miss my chance. I lunged forward and grabbed him, and we wrestled. I held him in a bearhug and wasn't going to let go. I squeezed with all my might until he couldn't breath and dropped to the floor. To make sure, I twisted his neck until it snapped. I left him under a pile of heavy, black moving blankets. What they did to me. I was willing to do anything to get free.

I took off right away and worked my way to my home. I was going to see Hannah again. My life, I hoped, would return to some kind of normal. I would explain, and she would understand. She would take me in her arms and cover me with kisses and say, "I love you, Jake. I missed you so much." It was night. I walked up the front walk as I always did then stopped and looked in the front window as I always had done. There she was pouring a cup of coffee. Then to my surprise she poured another. And there he was, detective Jon. He put his arms around her, and they embraced, held each other tight, squeezing the life out of me. Everything I had was taken from me. I was lost and alone. I ran into the enveloping darkness. I had taken money from the warehouse before I took off – a substantial amount – and took a cab and booked into a hotel on Kingston Road. In the *Toronto Star* a few days later, there was a mention of a murder at an east-end warehouse and linked it to an earlier murder of a man found in Lake Ontario. Both were known to the police as members of a criminal gang and were likely victims of gangland retribution. I couldn't go to the police and explain what had happened. To return to society with my identity, I would have to make up a story that I had been beaten and kidnapped by two people who took me north to Sioux Lookout, where I was held captive. When I wasn't locked alone in a small room, I was blindfolded and never saw them. The beating left me with amnesia which meant that they couldn't demand a ransom because I didn't know who I was or where I lived. They didn't want to kill me, so they left me in the woods outside of town, hoping I would perish and disappear. A trucker found me wandering along Highway 642 early one morning and picked me up. I told him I was working my way back to Toronto after being out west for some time. The kindness of strangers. He called some of his buddies who were driving rigs to Toronto. They took care of me. Within a week, I was back in the city.

The other thing I needed to be sure of was that I had an alibi for the murder of Gladys Crummley, the mystery writer. We were lovers before I met Hannah and had had a tempestuous relationship. She was a very good writer, and I admit I was jealous of her. What complicated our story was that we had the same publisher, Ari Grimm. She was number one on his publishing list. I had only one book out and was number, who knows, but down on the list. Sometime before all this happened, I went to see Gladys because Ari had rejected my new manuscript. I was hoping she could convince him to publish it after another round of editing. She refused and mocked me. I was furious and left. A day later, she was found floating face down in Lake Ontario, a hundred yards off Balmy Beach. They weren't going to pin that on me. I had alibis. I was at work with Spinelli, the bar owner, every night. I'm sure Hannah would vouch for me for other times. The police never found the murderer.

I'm free. Except for one thing. Al. He's still around, and I know he's looking for me. That's why I'm keeping low. I spend some time here at the café working on my new novel, *After Hannah*, or stay in my one-room flat in Cabbagetown. If he finds me, I'm dead. Unless something happens to him.

I still can't shake this feeling of restlessness that has been dogging me for so long. I never shared this with Hannah because I wasn't sure what it was. Now after everything I've gone through, I need to be honest with myself. It's not a mystery. I don't let myself get hung up on metaphysical questions like what am I doing here? Even when Hannah and I were together, even in our best moments, there was always something eating away at me. I couldn't shake the feeling that whatever I did, I was a fraud, and everyone knew it. The smiles were sneers, the tone derisive. Even that bastard, Ari Grimm, who made money from my novel mocked me. Once when I was in his waiting room before a meeting, I heard him talking on the phone with Gladys Crummley. They were constantly tittering and guffawing; then I heard Ari chortle, "He's in the waiting room." Rest in peace, Gladys. You'd better publish my new novel, Ari. Lake Ontario can be very cold.

Al saw me the other day. He followed me, but I lost him. I'm trying to remain unknown and unseen, lost to the world. I know too much. Then there's the money. I haven't counted it all, but there was a lot. I stuffed it all into a knapsack. As well, I took their accounting books. I've leafed through them. They're full of not-so-subtle accounting terminology that reflects the boys' business practice such as "May 3, 2k from Istvan. 8k to be paid by July 3, or we break his son's legs." Al won't rest until he finds me. The day after I saw him, I spotted crazy Jocasta on Queen Street near Broadview. They're sweeping the city. I imagine Jocasta sharpening her blade in anticipation of sticking me in the stomach and diaphragm. I never finished Hebrew school, and I don't remember much, but this directive from the Talmud has stuck in my mind all these years, if someone comes to kill you, rise up and kill him first.

I put the pages down, thinking that Jake had crossed the line between fiction and reality and had given what had happened to him away. What was his novel going to reveal? The more I thought about it, it just might be a brilliant strategy. It sounds so plausible that people would rush to read it as an authentic biography even as Ari Grimm packaged it as fiction. Jake will always claim that it's a work of fiction with a few elements taken from the nightly news.

18

This morning after breakfast as I was clearing the dishes and cups from the table, Abby came over to me and leaned her head on my shoulder. "You remember I gave my notice two weeks ago, don't you?" I told her that I did. "Well, this is my last day. We're going to be free to spend all our time together and do what we want." I was so happy to hear this I took her in my arms and lifted her up and twirled her around in a ragged, 360-degree circle, which I have to admit strained my back and made me a little dizzy. "Easy, my love," she said and steadied me. "I'm off to my last day of work." I hugged and kissed her at the front door. "I'll be here waiting for you, Abby."

Around 10 o'clock, I received a text message from Lorne asking me to meet him at the café. "I've asked Jake to meet us there." It's always the same, a good thing is followed by something dark. Why is that? I could feel the tentacles of depression tightening around me. I began to feel restless. I had hoped to begin the final chapter of my book. I was closing in on the final action and was looking forward to discovering what it would reveal. Then the doubt spilled over the manuscript as if an opened bottle of black ink had tipped over onto it. Who was really interested in what an aging writer managed to cobble together? As I read and reread the previous chapter, questions filled my mind to the point that I began to wonder if I was looking to find a reason to abandon the whole project. It doesn't take much for paralysis to tighten a clamp around the imagination. What was I hoping to accomplish anyway? I don't need the stress. I'll just leave it. I can begin a new story anytime. Just not today. In truth, Abby and I would be the only ones disappointed. The familiar anxiety and restlessness ran through me like a jagged current of electricity. I kept searching for a way back into the narrative. It was no use. I caved into the gloom. I used my meeting Lorne at the café as the excuse. I put my notes and pens in my satchel and went off to the café, feeling lousy.

Lorne was sitting at the table by the window looking onto Harbord Street. He pulled out a chair. "I'm happy to see you. How have you been?"

"Only so-so." I looked out at the flow of students walking to the campus.

"Are you having trouble dealing with –"

"Bloody West Beach?"

"Bloody Port Hope. He sent me his preface too."

"That and the end of my book. I just want to write The End and put it away."

"If it were only that easy. I'm stuck on what I thought would be part two of the story. After writing 20 pages, it became obvious that it wasn't at all the second part but rather an extension of a crucial thread from chapter 16. At least that's what I think today. It might be different tomorrow if I kill off one of the characters. If I have him incarcerated…. That might work. Give me a minute to think about that."

He unscrewed his fountain pen and began making notes. Couples with knapsacks and earphones stuck into their ears walked by holding hands on their way to classes or to the Robarts Library. What I wouldn't give to be able to relive those years. Even if the goal wasn't always clear, the purpose was. Every thought and action held the promise of endless possibilities. What the hell happened? I knew the answer only too well—age and the machine wearing out.

Jake burst through the door and came right over and plopped down on a chair. He was breathing heavily and sweating. "Jon, bloody detective Jon, goddamn detective Jon who stole my Hannah, confronted me on the street near my flat this morning."

Lorne and I stared at each other. "What did he want?" Lorne asked.

"He asked me where I've been, what I've been doing. 'You were a missing person. Why didn't you contact Hannah or the police?'"

I thought Jake was going to burst. "What did you tell him?"

"That I had been kidnapped and beaten. I had amnesia. I had no idea who I was or where I was. Then he tells me that Hannah's cousin saw me in a bar some months ago. Impossible, I told him."

"Easy Jake," Lorne said. "Breathe and tell us slowly. Could her cousin have seen you?"

"She might have when I was out one night collecting at a bar for the boys. I think Jon knows something."

"Why do you say that?" I asked. I didn't like where this was going. The early afternoon sun snuck behind a bank of clouds and cast a shadow through the window and across the table.

"Then Jon Boy asked me if I had ever been in a warehouse on Eastern Avenue. Of course, I denied it. 'No way,' I told him. Then the arrogant bastard said, 'We found your fingerprints all over the place there.'"

"Impossible," I told him.

"Prints don't lie, Jake."

"He called me, Jake. I wanted to...."

"We got yours from your house, when you lived with Hannah. Your prints are still all over there."

"Can you imagine the gall of the bastard? I wanted to clobber him right there. He didn't let it go. 'Do you know Al Pommeroy?' he asked."

"Never heard of him," I told him.

"Or his brother Dan Pommeroy?:

"I don't know either of them."

"I think you do. They're crooks who lived and worked out of the warehouse on Eastern Avenue where we found your prints. Both were murdered. Al Pommeroy was found floating in Lake Ontario off West Beach in Port Hope some time ago. Do you want to rethink what you're telling me?"

"No need to, I told him. "You're balmy."

"So where have you been all this time?" Jake.

"As I'm telling him, he's scratching away on a cheap notepad with a Bic. I told him the story about having amnesia, being taken up north, then being let go in the woods where I regained my memory. Then he asked, 'So why didn't you come back to Hannah. She was worried about you.'"

"Well, I did come back, Jon," I told him, "except when I walked up to the front steps and saw her in the kitchen, I also saw you. You took her in your arms and kissed her. It was clear what was going on, a clear breach of your professional ethics. I'll be writing a letter of complaint to your supervisor. See what he thinks of you then. He didn't flinch."

"Now that your memory has miraculously returned, Jake, don't leave the city. You'll be hearing from me again."

"Then he left."

He looked at us. "Do you have any ideas? Anything?" What should I do?"

19

I was out of ideas. I needed to put it all behind me and focus on Abby and this next step in our lives. We went through books, maps and itineraries and searched online for more information. Our freedom made us lightheaded as we spent days planning our escape. Finally, we looked at each other and said, "This is it." We were going to fly to Paris to see her cousin Yael, stay a week then fly to Israel and spend three weeks. I had a friend from McGill who had made aliya several years after his retirement who had tried to convince me to go with him. "Come on," he enticed me. "Let's change our lives, do something good for ourselves, go back to our roots." I wasn't ready then, and I'm not sure I am now even though it's only a short stay. Today, I have Abby, and the future looks promising, even as I am well into my seventies and feeling my age in my back and knees and more concerning in my mind. To be honest, I'm not as sharp as I was even two years ago. I sometimes have to search for words and can't find expressions or clarify ideas. That has been my whole life as a writer and professor. I try not think where this is going to end up.

A month before we left, I found an email from Lorne in my inbox.

Dear Jacob,
I hope you're well and that you're close to finishing your novel. How about coffee and a conversation in a new café? Our old haunt is compromised.

I wrote back telling him of our plans and that coffee would be great but received nothing back. Then a cryptic message followed.

I'm going to be away for some time. I'll let you know where I can be contacted. Please delete this after reading.

I did as he asked and wondered why the secrecy. Did he hear something? Was the detective harassing him? Two weeks after that, I received another email.

Am teaching a year at Yerevan University. Keep it to yourself. Accommodations are adequate and the food is good; Armenians are warm. I'm living like a monk. Teaching, eating, writing, a little rest, then the cycle begins once again the next day. I have a computer, access to a printer, and the coffee is great. The place is bristling with pent-up energy and desire. I may not return. Shalom."

A month later, I received another email.

My novel is finished and is being translated into Armenian. Go figure. It's a book, and it's going to be published. In Armenian. I know what you're thinking, but it's a book. It might be on the bestseller list in Armenia. It's a pity that things rarely work out for us as we had hoped. We're always making do until the next opportunity. It's a hell of a way. The university is always looking for good professors. Let me know if you're interested. You'd love it here. Remember, you don't know where I am.

We left Toronto in the evening with me wondering if I had packed everything I would need: my heart meds, enough fountain pens and ink, notebooks, clothes, and painkillers. I slept through most of the flight and was abruptly awakened after being severely jostled by turbulence. We were happy to land, and despite being a little wobbly going through customs, we made it into the city of light on a bright sunny morning. I was thankful for the cliché. I hadn't been in Paris since my second last sabbatical years ago. No matter how many times I've visited, it's always an amazing experience to walk through the city.

Yael greeted us with hugs and kisses and invited us to sit for a wonderful snack of croissants, cheese, fresh fruit and coffee during which she and Abby caught up on family news. I was happy to get to know more about Abby from the stories Yael told me. She was a former journalist, and as we were preparing to leave to visit the *Musée d'art et d'histoire du Judaïsme* in the Marais quarter near where she lived, she told us, "It's quite sad, but it's becoming more and more difficult for Jews to live in France."

As we walked through the various sections and displays in the museum, Abby took my hand and took me by surprise when she asked if I would like to visit Salonica. "You mean Thessaloniki," I said. She tried to convince me. "We're a short plane ride away. It would be a return, taking your family home." I remained silent. We walked through the Holocaust exhibit of how the Jews of Paris suffered and coped with the Nazi occupation and with the collaboration of the government. I could sense she was upset by my silence. My first instinct was to say no. I was a distant relative of Salonica separated by too much time, space and experience. She held my arm tightly as we walked slowly through the somber exhibits. We stopped, confronted by a wall of photographs of Jews being rounded up and pushed up onto trucks to be taken away to transit camps like Drancy. The fear was palpable on their faces as mothers held their children close, unsure of what was going to happen to them next but suspecting the worst. German soldiers in their drab uniforms wore their stone stares like rifles at the ready. I turned to Abby, "I do feel compelled to go and see the city and what remains of the Jewish community. There are only about a thousand Jews left. When my father was taken away with the first group to build roads soon after the Nazi occupation, there were fifty-four thousand in the city. From what I've read, maybe a dozen or so people still speak Ladino. The last generation to speak it as their every-day language were those who survived the Holocaust. However, fear of being targeted and pursued, forced them to stop speaking their native language. They told their children to speak Greek. I would not recognize the place my parents remembered and told me about. It would be too confusing and painful."

I wasn't even certain of how to speak of my parents' homeland. We visited Abby's remaining family in Paris. Much of the talk revolved around whether aging aunts and uncles would stay or leave for Israel. As we walked the city, we wondered if Jewish presence here would soon pass into history.

Yael prepared lunch and snacks for us to take on the plane for the five and-a-half-hour flight to Tel Aviv. I was uneasy, not only because I hate flying but for many of the same reasons that going to Thessaloniki made me feel. Coming to Israel would be a very late homecoming, well over 2,000 years late. My parents were Zionists before the war. If they had ever discussed going to pre-independent Israel, they never told me. The war ended any thoughts of that. Once in America, they put all their energy in re-establishing themselves. My father had a career as a teacher and a writer. And then I came along, and we all became North Americans.

After sightseeing and visiting museums during the day, we would spend late afternoons at a beachside café near our hotel talking about how vibrant the country and the people were despite the enormous pressure that exists every moment of the day for Israelis. One morning Abby took me to the cemetery where her husband is buried. She stood by the grave and brought me close to her as she said the mourner's *Kaddish*. She cried as she told me about Alon and their life together here that the Yom Kippur War destroyed. She took my arm and said, "He was a good man, Jacob. So many died so young." Walking out past all the graves, my mind was awash with so many thoughts and emotions. For much of my life, I kept myself at a distance from most things. I filtered everything through books and my profession. It was a safe way to live that allowed me to remain detached from how messy life can get. I didn't deal well with my parents' passing. I've never gotten over it and feel terribly guilty to this day that I wasn't with them more. Then there was my divorce from Devorah or rather her divorce from me. She deserved more than I was able to give her. Despite all our previous troubles, she helped me get through my heart surgery. I have only good feelings for her. I just feel so separated from everything except Abby. My world is shrinking.

It's 2:30 in the morning, and I'm looking out over the Mediterranean from our room in Tel Aviv. The moon falls softly on the water. I look at Abby sleeping soundly and give thanks for her presence. I owe her my life. I go to the writing

109

desk and open a notebook and wonder how I can ever express my love for her. I screw the cap off my fountain pen and write in capital letters the title of a poem I will begin here.

20

Once again, Abby tried to convince me to travel to Salonica. We had lost many members of our family taken from there to the death camp that was Auschwitz. It was hard to argue against that. I went silent and looked out the window as we plowed our way through the sky. "You want to avoid taking on the pain of your parents' experience," she said. "Whether you like it or not, you're the protector of their voices and memories." I wondered as I looked out over the banks of clouds extending far into the distance what meaning I could bring by going to Salonica. There remains little sign of pre-war Jewish life. "My going would not be a pilgrimage. I wouldn't be able to make the past present, Abby, nor would I find the past that happened there." She leaned her head on my shoulder. "I don't need to tell you this, my love. You need to find ways to make it present. Experiencing the absence will make you a witness. It's what we do every Passover. The Haggadah is all about bearing witness for later generations."

But what is being witnessed? I remember my father every night writing in his study. His desk was piled high with books and papers. I could hear his fountain pen skating furiously across the pages as he worked under the dull yellow light of his lamp. That sound will be with me forever. The morning I left to take up my first teaching job at the University of Toronto, he told me, 'Since the war, there will always be something missing from our lives that causes trauma and anxiety. In all the pages I have filled, I have tried to leave you, my son, some record of what can be known through my experience. But there will always remain so much of what cannot be known.' If I let myself be directed by my father's narratives of things I never experienced, they will become an absent memory; a regret will fill me for not having been there and lived through it. In his life, so much was emptiness and loss. In his world, there was a constant unsettledness, a restlessness. The process of mourning never ended. He knew what he had lost and grieved, but he was unable to move on. Some have written that the goal of those of the second generation, those born after the war, is to find the lost object that has caused the mourning. In his case it was Salonica. While I lament the pain and loss, I have chosen not to mourn. As I have aged, every day I fight against the fragmentation and displacement of my life. Every morning is a challenge to face and resist the dissipation of my life. I wonder how much longer I have.

I looked over at Abby who had nestled into me and had fallen into a delicious sleep. I thought of my father's papers and books untouched after the *Shiva*. My mother left the mourners and asked me to follow her into his study. She opened one of the desk drawers and took out my father's fountain pen. "This is for you. He always wanted you to have it." She then took out a package sealed in an envelope. "This was his final work before he left us. You should take it with you, Jacob." When Abby and I returned home, I went to my desk and sat. I uncapped my father's pen and wrote with it. It was still filled with his favourite blue-black in. I recapped the pen and put it on my desk. I was somewhat nervous about taking out the notebook. What was he working on when his heart failed? I pulled back the hard, black cover and saw that on the first page, he had written a dedication.

To my son Jacob with my love and respect.
Your father

I admit that I broke down. I wiped away the tears and opened the first page. There was only one word, "I." That's all he wrote. It was clearly his intention, but what was it? What was he telling me? What did he want me to know?

I've been thinking about this for years. Abby's questioning why I didn't want to go to Salonica triggered something that has helped me understand my father and my relationship to him. By writing "I" as he did in his last work, he was calling attention between narration and survival. His surviving made it necessary for him to recount it, to be heard in order for him to survive. However, the more I thought about it, he wasn't just telling his story. The "I" of his stories is his search for a "you," for someone he could address. In his final work, my father was telling me that there can be no witness, an "I" without a "you," that is, in this case, his son. He was compelling me to be a witness to his witnessing. In re-reading all his work since the war, I can see that my father in addressing me has made me a participant and also a co-owner of the traumatic events he and my mother lived through. This is why it was so important for my father that I read his work and comment on it. When I began developing my own career and no longer paid the same amount of attention to the Holocaust and Salonica, it pained him. Each new work he sent me was a reminder and a call to listen. He needed me to be his witness, the caretaker of his memories. Abby knew this better than I did. I didn't go to Salonica, but I am reading through my father's many books and published essays again. I have become his witness. At 73, how will this change me?

21

I had been struggling to find the ending of my novel, now 300 double-spaced pages on the computer taken from over 1,000 handwritten sheets lying in an archive box. Night had fallen hours ago. I left Abby sleeping soundly and quietly went to my writing room and opened my black Leuchtturm notebook. I unscrewed the cap of my dark grey *Marlen Giornale* fountain pen and began writing, free associating, trying to conjure an event, perhaps a surprise that will push the action towards a conclusion. I thought of Lorne sipping dark Armenian coffee late in the night in Yerevan. He fills his pen with blue-black ink and makes notes for a new story slowly taking shape after the success of his Armenian novel, as he calls it. He thinks about calling this one *West Beach*, a story of friendship, naïve intentions and murder, a literary murder story of rejection, hopes dashed and revenge. And finally, self-imposed exile. It's only 1:30 am. The couple across the corridor from Lorne are having a party. American rock and roll seeps through under the door. From the apartment above where his colleague, a musicologist from Los Angeles lives, the sad, sweet folk music of Armenia rises and falls then hauntingly disappears. Does Lorne hear it?

I can't avoid a dilemma that's been eating at me for some time. I need to tell Abby about the events that led us to Port Hope. If I tell her, it will surely provoke a crisis, and I could lose her. If I don't tell her, I will have to live with the dishonesty that will affect our relationship. I'm trying to be a better person. I want to be rid of this restlessness that has unsettled me even before I left Montreal. I don't think I'll ever be free of it. I keep hearing my father quoting Rabbi Nachman of Breslov, "If you are not a better person tomorrow than you are today, what need have you for a tomorrow?" After our Shabbat meal, my father would ask me to come with him to his study after I helped my mother clear the table. We would sit together and talk. He was never a dogmatic person who would insist that as Jew one has to act in such a way. Rather his lessons were short and to the point. I called them life lessons. On one Shabbat, I complained about something; no doubt it was trivial but seemed important to me. "Jacob," he said, "the purpose of our lives is to improve our characters by working on ourselves every day. That's why God has given us today and tomorrow." Dear Father and Mother, how I miss you both. You knew I had to strike out on my own, to find my own way. When I left, you knew that nothing would ever be the same. Yet it was something that had to happen.

I confess. To everything. Abandoning my parents, causing Devorah to leave me, hurting many during my career, letting Al Pommeroy die. I know that confessing to one thing opens the door to many others. But having admitted wrongdoing, I don't feel any sense of rehabilitation or the beginning of a re-entry into the human community. There is no commensurate punishment given except for the constant feeling of being ill at ease, restless. Off balance. There is no ritual offering absolution or reintegration. I confess. I'm struggling against the tyranny of transparency because it eliminates all areas of privacy. The logic demands that the only way to clean one's conscience is to make it accessible to everybody. There must be no spaces of obscurity. I'm waiting to see if telling the truth has a therapeutic value. I confess, Abby.

After several troubling months, Jake sent me an advanced copy of *After Hannah* that Ari Grimm had published. Already the critical reviewing mafia were calling for it to be awarded the "Black Trillium" award for the best crime fiction by an Ontario writer. Inside the front cover was a handwritten note asking that we meet at the *Waterman Bookstore Café* next Tuesday at 10:00 am. I sent him a message letting him know I'd be there.

I looked forward to seeing him and congratulating him on his success. Lorne also had received an advanced copy and phoned from Yerevan to wish Jake well. The message ended with, "All good here. No plans to return just yet."

I left the house around nine as I planned to walk down Avenue Road to Hoskins Avenue past the university then along to Harbord Street a few blocks west to the café. The streets were busy as usual with students. I was looking forward to an espresso and hearing how Jake was enjoying his success. I pushed open the door and stumbled over the threshold but managed to catch myself before I went tumbling on the floor. Harold, the owner, looked over smiled. "The usual, Jacob?" I nodded. There were a few people in at that hour. I sat at the table by the window and took out my pen and notebook from my backpack and started making notes. Through the window, I saw Jake approaching. As he was about to cross the street and come to the café, a woman in her late forties with long, red hair falling down her back pulled Jake's shoulder from behind. When he stopped and faced her, she began screaming at him. There within the frame of the window I saw both pairs of arms flailing at each other as things escalated out of control. Then I realized it was Jocasta O'Brien, Al Pommeroy's girlfriend. I got up to go to Jake's aid when she pulled out a dagger from her bag and stabbed him in the stomach and in the back. Three students who were passing by held her down and subdued her. She was still out of control by the time I got to Jake. She kept yelling, "He and his friends killed my man! I'm going to kill them all!" One of the students said he already called for an ambulance and had taken photos with his phone for the police.

Even as the police officers were putting Jocasta in the back of their car, she continued screaming, "It was for Al! He and his friends killed him! I'll get them all!" I stayed with Jake until the ambulance came, but he had bled profusely and had gone into shock and lost consciousness. I don't know if he had recognized me. One of the paramedics told me they were taking him to Saint Michael's Hospital on Bond Street. Four squad cars arrived as well as the crime scene unit. Officers took everyone's name including mine and began going over the area and collecting information.

The students continued on their way to classes, and the rest of the crowd dispersed. I was stunned and stood on the corner, wondering what I should do. Finally, it occurred to me that I should go to see Jake. I gathered my things from the café then started walking east then south to College Street then over to Yonge Street. On my way to the hospital, I began wondering about the wisdom of what I was doing. The police will investigate Jocasta's claim about Al. Detective Jon already has doubts about Jake and me. He'll get word of what had happened and will begin digging deeper into Al Pomeroy's murder. What might he find that would link us to Al? Was I being careful or being a coward? This thought refused to go away but remained like a needle stuck in the brain stirring things up, causing pain and worry.

117

22

Abby was noticeably agitated as I cleared the table after supper, so much so that she closed the door of the dishwasher with a thud. I looked over at her, "What was that about?"

"You tell me what's going on, Jacob. You've been acting strange for days now. There's something bothering you, and you're shutting me out."

Abby had never spoken to me that angrily. I couldn't just come out and tell her. Like the coward I am, I spoke around what was happening. I wove a story that had just enough elements of the truth to be plausible, but not enough to keep me from being a liar. For the first time, I wasn't being honest with Abby, and I hated myself for it.

We sat on the couch, and I told her about Jake's success with his new novel. I told her the story is based in part on the fact that he had been kidnapped a year or so ago and that the detective on his missing person's case, Jon, started a relationship with his wife given that Jake had disappeared. There had been no word from him or about him in all that time. Hannah, and Jon, the detective, began living together in Jake and Hannah's house. I explained that Al, Dan and Soren had sequestered Jake and had forced him into participating in their criminal activities until he managed to get free. On the evening of his escape, he went up the front walk of their place and saw through the front window his wife and Jon embracing.

He ran and hid and lived off the money he had stolen from the crooks who had held him.

"Why didn't Jake go to the police or contact his wife?" It was the obvious question, but logic wasn't at work here. I wasn't sure she believed me or thought I was making it all up.

"This is where it gets even more complicated," I told her. "You see in order to escape from the gang, he had to kill two of them. He took all their money from the extortions they had committed. So, if he had gone to the police, he would have to admit to killing two people and using their ill-gotten gains."

I was at the moment when I had to decide whether to continue and tell her everything or continue hiding the rest of the story from her, the part that involves me. She got up to make us espresso. As the machine pumped out two cups, one after the other, she said something, but I didn't hear because of the noise. I could have used that break to end the story, and had I been quicker, I might have; however, when Abby returned and sat beside me, she said, "You haven't told me how you're involved in all this."

"What do you mean?" I was grasping at anything that might help me avoid continuing. I sipped the espresso slowly and played with the cup and saucer.

"We'll you've been meeting Jake and Lorne at *Waterman's Bookstore Café* for some time now. Surely, you talk about more than your works in progress. Has he asked for your help?"

"He asked me to read his preface a while ago and give him some feedback."

"That's all? I would have thought that someone with his history would need help reintegrating. How is he?"

Here was an opening to talk around the story without delving deeper into what went wrong. "He's okay. At least he was okay." I just wanted to go and lie down. There was no way

I was going to get out of this. If I were to tell Abby everything, what would she think of me? If I didn't, I would be deceiving her and compromising our relationship.

"What happened, Jacob?"

"Well the good news is that Jake's novel has been nominated for the Black Trillium Prize for the best work of crime fiction this year. *After Hannah* is about his kidnapping and how he escaped. It's a good novel. Ari Grimm is publishing it. A week ago, when I went to the café to meet Jake, I saw him get attacked and stabbed on the street beside Waterman's. He's in bad shape, but he'll recover. I've gone to see him at the hospital a couple of times."

"That's quite a story. I'm glad he's going to be okay. He's lucky to have you and Lorne as his friends. Where is Lorne in all of this? You haven't mentioned him at all."

I was feeling worse by the minute. "Lorne is teaching at the University of Armenia in Yerevan for the year. An Armenian publisher there has published his novel, *In Plain Sight.* He likes it there; he says there's a good writing community."

"It's your turn now, my love. Your book will be out very soon."

"I have to finish it first."

"You will. You have all your time to do it. So tell me, who attacked Jake? What was the motivation?"

"I don't know. The police are still investigating." Okay, I thought, I dodged one. Now, I can relax and focus on the final chapter. I sat back and sighed. Then Abby said, "I forgot to tell you, Jacob. Someone named Jon called you today. He said you know him. He'll call you tomorrow." It was as if Abby had poured bitters in my coffee.

I knew that if I tried to put off meeting Detective Jon, it would only make him more tenacious and make me appear guilty of whatever he suspected me of doing. When he called, I knew I was in for the intimidation treatment as he asked me to come to his office at 53 Division at 75 Eglinton Avenue West. I had never been to a police station before, and when I opened the door at the front entrance, I had more than a few butterflies in my stomach. Just stick to the story, I kept telling myself. I had gone over it many times the night before. I know Jake and Lorne from the café. No, I have never been to Port Hope. Yes, I was nervous.

Fifty-three Division was a solid-looking reddish-brown brick building with the entrance cut at a 45-degree angle at the intersection. I went in and looked around and saw people asking questions at a counter up ahead. A cheerful officer asked how he could help me. I told him about my appointment. He went to his computer to check. "Oh, yes, he left a message for you. He's in Port Hope this morning, at West Beach with a forensic unit. You'd be surprised what these people can find buried in the sand or caught on a branch or rock. He'll call you."

I left feeling worse than I did when I entered. I needed to speak to Jake so I took the subway down to Queen Street then walked over to Saint Michael's Hospital. I went up to Jake's room and found there were several journalists and a camera crew around his bed filming the new winner of the Black Trillium Award. Jake saw me and gave me a nod. "I'll call you later," he said. I wondered whether I should go home and tell Abby to pack her bag; we're going to Salonica. I needed to get away from the city, Port Hope and West Beach. But of course, I didn't. I went to the café and took out my notebook and unscrewed the cap of my black Pilot 823. I began making notes relating to that fateful night that led us to West Beach and the cold water of Lake Ontario. I needed to outline the story to clarify it in my mind if only to save my sorry soul against whatever Detective Jon might find hiding on the beach. Once I had done that, I turned to my father's final words, his desire to bind me to our heritage and our fate. After struggling with this for several hours, I went home. Abby welcomed me with a long hug and kiss. "Come, my love. I've made soup for you." I washed up and came back to the table happy to see Abby again. She put the bowl of vegetable soup before me. "Detective Jon called an hour ago."

"My God, will no one rid me of this meddlesome detective?" My outburst surprised her.

"Jake, why are you reacting this way?"

"Sorry, I was channeling Henry II."

"Well, my love, I don't get it. What's his interest in you anyway, Jacob?"

"I saw Jake getting stabbed. I guess he wants to go over my statement."

"Well, he asked me to tell you that he has just returned from Port Hope and wants to see you at the café tomorrow at 10 am. You can call him if you can't. He mentioned West Beach. What does West Beach have to do with Jake's stabbing?"

"No idea," I lied. I looked away and picked up my spoon and began eating. "Your soup is delicious, Abby."

She smiled and sat down across from me and watched me eat.

23

Before entering the café, I looked through one of the windows and saw Detective Jon sitting at the table where Jake, Lorne and I usually sat, talking to Harold, the owner. He was jotting down a few notes in a small black hardcover book with the same orange BIC he was using before. Every few seconds he shook the pen hard to force the ink to flow onto the page. Then to my surprise, he pulled from his bag a copy of *After Hannah* and began thumbing through pages he had marked with green flags. I began to feel apprehensive and walked around out front to gather my thoughts before entering when the front door to the café suddenly swung open. "I thought it was you," he said. "Come in. Apparently, you like decaf espresso. I've ordered us two."

I sat quietly and let him talk. His eyes were focused on my reactions as I made an effort not to have any. "We found certain items on the beach, West Beach, yesterday. People aren't always aware of what they lose or what is left by them. For example, we found a belt loop from the pants Al Pommeroy was wearing the night he was murdered." His stare burned into me when he said this. I remained still. "And there was a gold money clip with a Hebrew letter on it, a yod. Pardon my pronunciation. You must still know Hebrew, Jacob or is it Yaacov?"

I told him that I still remembered the alphabet.

"So then, what do you think the letter on the clip might stand for, Yaacov?"

"My name is Jacob, Jon. I don't use my Hebrew name. I have no idea. The letter could stand for anything."

"It is odd, don't you think, that we found the clip with a Hebrew letter on it at West Beach."

"You seem surprised that Jews like to sun on a beach and swim. Perhaps it was there from last season. There is a Jewish congregation just down the road in Oshawa."

He put the clip in his pocket. "Let's put aside this item for now. I went back to the morgue to check Pommeroy's body. There are bruises on his body likely from people trying to lift or drag the body. As well, there are a series of marks around his throat as if someone was trying to strangle him. The autopsy showed that he was killed elsewhere, not at the beach as there was no water in his lungs. There were fibres found on his shirt perhaps from the car that brought him to the beach or from the shirt of one of the killers before they disposed of him in the lake."

"Why are you telling me this? Am I a suspect?"

"No. I'm just trying to see if the clues add up. We're looking into all of this and more. What they tell us will help us make a case against the killers."

"Why do you say 'killers'?"

"It's just an impression at this point."

I tried to bring the discussion back to Jake but ended up walking into it. "Have you found anything relating to the attack on my friend?"

"Jake? Yes, we have. The woman who stabbed him is Jocasta O'Brien. Do you know her?"

"Never heard of her." The corners of his mouth went into a half smile.

"It turns out that she was Al Pommeroy's girlfriend. Imagine that."

I should have stopped there, but no, I had to engage. It was as if all my years as a professor debating and arguing with students and colleagues had now led me to debate myself into suspicion. "What could have been her motive?"

"Well," Jon said, pausing for a moment for dramatic effect, "she claims that Jake killed her boyfriend, Al Pommeroy."

"Why would Jake do that? Did they even know each other?" Here, he opened Jake's novel. "According to his story, the gang who kidnapped him could have been Pommeroy's crew, a two-bit bunch that grifted mostly but not exclusively in the east end of the city." Jon was really enjoying this.

"May I remind you, detective," I said, trying to gain the upper hand, "that Jake's novel is fiction. Invented. Made up."

"Fiction, friction. Granted," Jon said dismissively, "but I am well placed to know part of the truth of Jake's story. I married his former wife. Jake disappeared for some time. Where was he? According to his story, he was taken by a gang. Which gang. Who?"

"It's fiction detective. A story. One that is so well written it won an award."

"There's more here than meets the eye. Give me time."

After a moment of silence, he rubbed his chin and asked, "And what's your relation to all of this?"

"I'm working on a novel. Jake and I often meet here to discuss the progress we're making."

"And who is Lorne?"

"Another writer. One of our group."

"He's in Armenia now, isn't he?"

"Yes." I was surprised he knew this and wondered what other surprises he was waiting to spring on me. "We've been out of touch for some time."

He put his notes and Jake's novel back into his bag and rose. "Thank you for your cooperation. I may have to contact you again so let me know if you plan to leave town."

Now, I was getting angry and he knew it. "Do you mean I can't leave town?"

"Not at all. It's just in case we need to speak to you to confirm things."

He left the café and left me puzzled and angry. I needed fresh air and decided to walk home even though my lower back was very sore. I needed time to gain some composure and come up with a plan on how I was going explain this to Abby.

24

A week later, the doctor told Jake that he was out of danger and released him five days later. I went to help him gather his things and got a cab to take him home. I had stocked his fridge and pantry a few days earlier and made him a simple pasta dish for supper. While he was eating, Ari Grimm called then the president of the Black Trillium Prize Committee phoned to say that now that Jake was on the mend, the ceremony would take place in a week at the Indigo Bookstore on Bay and Bloor. Jake was still quite sore from the surgeries but was happy. "It's the first time I've won anything for my writing, Jacob," he laughed. "Ari Grimm is thrilled. The book is flying off the shelves." I told him he should tell me if he needed anything. "I'll see you during the week and will pick you up at six the night of the ceremony." He thanked me and said he wanted to rest. As I was about to leave, he said that Jocasta O'Brien was still claiming that he had killed Al Pommeroy. She has no proof, but Detective Jon is still listening to her. He visits her in her cell every few days to see if there is a clue she might let slip he could use against me. "We have to stick to the story, Jacob." I told Jake that Detective Jon had asked about Lorne and that I had told him that he is happy in Armenia and hard at work on a new book. He's found an audience there just as you have one here now. "You know what they say is true, Jacob, you're only as good as your next book. Even in Armenia. I'm feeling the pressure already."

"Just enjoy the moment, Jake," I told him as if I were a sage. "How many good ones do we get? I'll call you tomorrow." I went home to Abby, wondering how wise I would be if we didn't get past this?

As we sat down to supper, Abby told me that Detective Jon had called. He was really getting on my nerves, but that's what he wanted to do so that I'd panic and screw up and say something that might implicate us. "What did he want?" I asked, forcing myself to appear calm.

"He didn't ask about you. He asked me if I had ever been to West Beach in Port Hope."

"And what did you tell him?"

"That I've never been, of course."

"He's really becoming annoying, but there's nothing we can do while the investigation into why that crazy woman stabbed Jake continues."

"I'm glad he's okay. It could have been very bad; an inch either way might have finished him."

"I'll check on him tomorrow. He's really looking forward to the award. It's worth ten thousand dollars and many book sales."

"I wish the same for you, my love." She caressed my cheek and kissed me softly.

Luck has never favoured me. Given all that's happened, I can't really complain. I have Abby.

"I'll go with you when you visit Jake tomorrow. I'll check on how he's doing and if he needs any medical attention."

I thanked her and held her in my arms and attempted a fancy two-step followed by a twirl. I banged into the grey sofa and began to list to the right. I was about to go over, but Abby held me tight. "I've got you, Jacob." I was wrong. Luck has favoured me.

25

The awards ceremony was well attended by writers hoping to be seen and written about by the literary journalists as well as those in the publishing world in the province. Carson Rathburn, the President of the jury came over to Jake and introduced himself. Jake urged him to shake his hand carefully as he was still in some pain. "So glad you came out of it all right, Jake," he said. "There's so much more we're expecting from you." Jake very kindly mentioned to him that I was putting the finishing touches on a new novel that will be a great success. "Well," he said, "I certainly look forward to reading it," then turned and went over to a cluster of well-known writers including two Governor General Award winners. I thanked Jake. "We have to milk every moment, Jacob." At that moment, Detective Jon, who had been moving around the room listening and observing those in attendance, came up behind Jake and startled him. "My, my," he said enjoying his tactic, "you must be guilty of something to have reacted that way. "Not at all, Detective. I'm a little shy when people come up behind me. You never know if they're clutching a shiv in their hand." Detective Jon opened his hands. "Nothing hidden. See."

"Are you enjoying the evening, Detective?" I asked.

"Very much. I'm learning a lot."

"Perhaps you're researching material for a book."

"Oh, I have lots of material. One of my most intriguing cases, the most intriguing perhaps, is the one concerning

Gladys Crummley. You must remember her, Jake. You were quite close at one time, weren't you?"

"It was a terrible loss for the literary community in the country."

"You should know, Jake, that I've kept the file open as a cold case. Something will turn up. I'll let you know when it does."

Jake turned away and pulled me away to join a group of writers we both knew. "By the way, Jake," Jon said, "Hannah passes on her congratulations. She's proud of you. She knew you'd make it."

"Why didn't she come and tell me herself?" Jake asked.

"She felt it would have been awkward. I'm sure you understand."

"Awkward for whom, detective?"

Jake received strong applause when he was called up to accept his award. Carson Rathburn concluded his remarks by reminding everyone that the literary profession can be dangerous. "Just ask Jake." More applause was joined with choruses of "Bravo, Jake!" I kept hearing Jake's remark, "You have to milk every moment," but I began to feel a little queasy. I went to get a drink and stood off to one side and assumed my usual stance of that of an observer. I was enjoying just being alone and watching everyone, but then Ari Grimm came over. Okay, I had to sell myself.

"Do you mind talking shop for a while?"

"I welcome to the opportunity."

"Can you give a brief overview of your story and characters?"

"Sure, Ari, I can do that." I summarized the whole thing, even embellished some." After ten minutes, he stopped me and asked me to send him my manuscript. "First thing tomorrow. I'll bring it over myself."

"Swell, Jacob. I look forward to reading it."

And that's how I got my break.

I helped Jake put his coat on and drove him back to his place. "Where did you put the check, Jake?"

"It's right here, deep in my pocket. Tomorrow it goes into the bank. Before too long, the royalties should begin rolling in. It's my time, Jacob. It may never happen again, but my name is on the award's list and they can't take that away from me. With some luck, this book will remain on the publishing lists for some time, along with translations in many languages. If I write nothing else or never get another book published, I'll always have this time to look back on with joy or with anger and frustration. But all that's for later. Come in for a drink. I'll get you an uber to take you home."

26

Three weeks had gone by without a word from Grimm, the Grim Reaper. I couldn't focus on the notes I was preparing for my next book that loomed like a dark cloud in my mind. Just this morning I recalled a moment that happened years ago after a seminar I had given on the literature of genocide. Rachel Rosenbaum, a quiet student who rarely offered an opinion during class came to my office to say how much she had found my book on the subject very helpful. She had lost family during the Shoah as had many of my students in other genocides, Armenian, Greek, Ukrainian and Rwandan. She was a tall woman with long, straight black hair and dressed rather soberly wearing a long, straight dark blue skirt and a white blouse and flat black shoes. Most of my students dressed in the eclectic fashion of the time. Rachel appeared as if she were going to a choir recital. "Excuse me, sir," she said timidly. "I just wanted to say that I found your study on the literature of genocide eye-opening, particularly your comparative approach and methodology. I've almost completed my essay on second-generation poetry after the Armenian Genocide and the Holocaust as witness literature." I told her I looked forward to reading it. At the end of the semester, she asked me to write her a letter of recommendation for a position in Jewish Studies she was seeking at a university in the States. I was always grateful to learn that my work had a positive effect on my students and colleagues. That moment passed, and I was back to stressing over my manuscript. I wanted to call Ari or ask Jake also but thought it wise not to. "Be calm, Jacob," Abby said softly. "Stressing won't change a thing except your health. Let's go down to the Beach and walk along the boardwalk." She saved me once again.

Four days later, I received a call from Grimm asking me to meet him the next day in his office at 10 am. I felt like a kid being summoned before the principal. Do we ever grow up?

I knocked on his door at 10 am sharp. He shouted for me to enter. His lair was a confusion of books, piles of papers on three tables, his desk and chair, a coffee maker, two computers, and an old, red armchair that engulfed me and held me in a firm grip when I sat.

"So, your manuscript," he said without raising his head. "First of all, you need a new title. Now, the awkward and the bad. There are too many digressions that are external and not relevant to the central theme, the idea, the crux of what you're working towards. The reason you are writing this thing. I know you're a professor and have a lot of ideas you want to throw in. You have to fight this compulsion. It gets in the way. Now, the good stuff. The interplay between the two generations of the family, now that is compelling." He pounded the desk with his fist. "Our generation, we live with our parents' nightmares. How can they be reconciled? Can there be any resolution, or does it all fall apart and the murderers win? If you rewrite your story with this in mind, and I like it, I'll put it on our Hanukah-Christmas books forthcoming list. I'd like to have you and Jake part of the Grimm stable of writers. Who knows, we may even make a few dollars." He looked at a large calendar on the wall behind him with names and number scratched all over it in red. "Okay, if you get it to me by mid-June, and I like it, we can begin to turn it into a book and an e-book and start the ad campaign. What do you say?"

"I'll put it in your hands by mid-June." What else could I say?

27

On June 1, I put my reworked manuscript in my bag and walked down to Grimm Publishing on College Street west of Bay and put it in Ari Grimm's hands. "What already? I didn't think you were going to make it." He flipped through the pages. "You've augmented it. A lot. And the title?" He went to the title page and looked at it. He thought quietly for a moment then nodded. "Good. Okay. This will do for now. We'll come back to the title later." I had questions but couldn't get a word in. "Leave it with me. I'll spend a few days with it then pass it on to the editorial board. We'll get back to you. It's a process. You have to be patient." He saw the look in my eyes. "Ten days. Give us ten days, Jacob. I'll call you."

I descended the stairs to College Street somewhat buoyed. I guess I was hoping to dance down the flight of stairs like Gene Kelly or Fred Astaire with a large smile lighting up my face as I landed a big ending. That's never going to happen. It's always joy deferred.

That night after supper, Abby brought me a sweater and said, "Let's walk. You need some distraction. We're not going to mention your novel or Ari Grimm." She took my arm, and we walked down to Prince Arthur then over to Bedford and down to Bloor Street where we got lost in the early summer evening crowds going in and out of the cafés, restaurants and shops selling items from all over the world. The city, my city now, was a multicultural delight, and Abby and I were happy to be a part of it.

When we returned home, Abby picked up the book she was reading and sat on the couch and began reading. I leaned forward to kiss her then headed for my writing room to check a notebook my father had left me. I had glanced at a particular passage several times but never took the time to go through it in depth. Now, looking at it closely, I could see it was a summation of what my parents had lived in their escape from home.

"I'm writing this for you, Jacob, so that our story will become part of your memory and also be a warning. This single incident was a key moment that saved our lives. It occurred in late June 1944, only a few months before the Battle for Marseilles that began on August 20, 1944. A small fishing boat we had hired in a fishing village in Italy had left us off on the coast near Marseilles. It was hard to look inconspicuous carrying our suitcases as we walked through the small town, looking for food and a place to stay. As we came out of a dark ally, we found ourselves surrounded by five armed men and a woman. Their leader asked who we were and what we were doing there. We couldn't know if they would turn us in. In that moment, I had to make a decision. I looked at your mother and saw the fear in her eyes. I explained that we were refugees escaping Nazi persecution in Salonica where most of the community had already been sent to Auschwitz. "*Vous êtes juifs.* You're Jews," the leader stated and looked over to his group. If I had lied and they searched our suitcases, they would have found our papers and the few remaining personal effects and quickly discovered who we were. They might not trust us. Who knows what they would have done to us? "*Suivez-nous,*" the leader said, "Come with us," and they walked us across the town square and down a narrow street that ran beside a church.

137

The imposing stone wall would make an appropriate place for an execution, I thought. The leader told us to stop then looked at his men then back at us. *"N'ayez pas peur. Vous êtes saufs.* Don't be afraid. You're safe," he said. Our lives were in his hands. He moved us to an alcove where the leader knocked on a door. A nun opened the door and saw our pitiful state. *"D'autres refugiés, ma soeur."* She took Rose's arm and gently guided her into the church. I followed, then turned around to thank the men, but they had already disappeared into the night. Soeur Marie took us down into the depths of the cellar of the old church. *"Vous devez avoir faim.* You must be hungry." She asked us to put down our suitcases and to sit at a small table with four rickety wooden chairs around it. Soeur Marie left us. Rose leaned against me. We were fatigued, famished and unsure of our fate. The politics in France was uncertain. We must have slept for a good while. When we opened our eyes, a priest was sitting at the table that now had two bowls of hot soup, cheese and bread on it. The priest, Père Jean, told us he had studied at a seminary in Jerusalem in the 30's and had made Jewish friends. "We can arrange passage on a boat to take you to Lisbon," he said. He handed me a slip of paper. "Memorize this address." After a minute, he took back the paper and burned it. "Once in the city, go there; someone will help you find a ship to Brazil. Eventually you will get to America. It will be long and difficult, but you must not lose hope." I told your mother that the circle will be complete. After the Inquisitions that drove Sephardic Jews out of Spain and Portugal to the Ottoman Empire, two are now returning. At least for a while.

"Before leaving, Father Jean and Sister Marie told us to eat and rest. "We will wake you in a few hours to start you on your journey," the father said. "Good luck. *Shalom.*" That was the last we saw of them. Two men from the group that found us the previous evening took us to board a ship that was anchored at a quay in harbour away from the town. They smiled and wished us *bonne chance* as we somewhat feebly climbed the gangplank up to the deck. A young sailor was waiting for us. He waved to our escorts then took us below. It was at that moment we knew we had a chance at survival. The Torah, in *Devarim*, Deuteronomy 10: 18-19, says "You too must love the stranger, for you were strangers in the land of Egypt." Many people risked their lives for us. A few robbed us along the way it has to be said. Eventually, after other clandestine voyages, we arrived in America four years after the war had ended. Jewish organizations helped us with little or no aid from governments."

I read this passage several times and studied it as I might a Torah portion. I placed my fingers on my father's text and heard him and my mother calling out to me. Jacob, our son, be our witness to the world. Let people know that we survived.

"I have to admit, my son, that through it all, I faltered several times; I weakened more than once and almost got us captured, but your mother, my beloved Rose, urged, forced me to continue. If we are alive today, it is because of her."

I recalled as a boy then as a teenager that my parents never told me of their escape and survival. My friends in school had family stories from Europe. When I asked, my father deflected. He never told me outright. From my bedroom at night, I could hear them whispering or talking low. "Maybe we should tell him, Shalom." They never did. They wanted me to have a clean slate. But how was that possible? I grew up and started my career as a professor and moved away and married Devorah. I should have stayed and cared for them after all they gave me. This is a guilt I will always carry.

Two weeks later, Ari Grimm called to say, "*Mazal tov!* We're going to publish your novel." I should have been happy or at least happier. My book was going to be released on Monday, December 23, the day after the first night of Hanukkah with yet another title. Ari liked the nervous, frenetic energy of the story and came up with *Restlessness*. I was okay with that. It certainly summed up what I've been feeling since my retirement and the bypass surgery, restlessness.

In the weeks that followed, the in-house production staff, four people including Grimm's nephew Isaac, who had graduated in graphic arts at Humber College, completed the production. I was actually surprised and pleased by the quality of his work. The copy editor had taken my biography and had worked it into a pithy and punchy text for the back cover under a mercifully flattering photo of me. I felt the rendering of the story line and characters didn't give enough information. "You're selling it short, Ari," I told him. "It's a teaser, Jacob. We don't want to give too much away. Let the reader put down twenty-five dollars then discover your talent." Talent, I thought. I don't know how the story got written. I felt unconscious through a lot of it. "The dedication to your parents is moving," Ari said. "Now, are you working on something new? We need product ready in case *Restlessness* takes off." I started telling him about my idea for the new story, but he cut me off. "Just get it ready, in case." I think I'll call the next one *Stressfulness*. I began seeing a whole series by Jacob Levy, any noun followed by -ness. And the Nobel Prize for Literature this year is awarded to Jacob Levy. A phone call from Abby brought me back to reality.

I gathered my notes and pens and was about to leave when Ari told me to begin working on my speech for the launch. "Keep it short. Thank Grimm Publishing, your parents and Abby, and make sure to mention that you're hard at work on your next novel. I'll call you to come in and see how the ad campaign is going. We'll set up interviews on tv and radio as well print media."

I went home to Abby elated and confused. As always, she put it all in context. "You worked hard for this, my love. Your moment has arrived; you have to be prepared to seize it. It may be the beginning of something important or something less, but you have to take it just as Jake embraced his moment." Bless you, Abby.

A week later, I got a phone call from Lorne, who said that he was going to be returning from Armenia in a week with his wife, a baby boy, and a third novel, a political thriller titled, *Republic Square, Yerevan*. Abby and I went to meet them at Pearson Airport, and when they came through the frosted glass doors at the arrivals area, his young wife was holding his arm, and he had a big grin on his face as he was pushing his baby in a stroller. After hugs and kisses, we all piled into an airport limo to take us back into the city. The three of us were back together again, and we needed to talk as Detective Jon had sent me an email three days earlier, stating that he has found new evidence in the Al Pommeroy murder and that we may be called in to the station for further questioning. I didn't even have time to enjoy the excitement surrounding the publication of my book. Maybe we should all go to Armenia, but as it happened, Armenia came to us. Lorne had now returned after almost a two-year absence during which he had written two political thrillers that were translated into Armenian and had become best sellers in the country. Lorne was exuberant and obviously happy to be back and introduce us to his family. He enjoyed recounting stories of his stay in Armenia. His wife Lucine was a translator for *Nor Or*, New Day Publishing, house that was bringing contemporary literature from around the world to Armenians as well as publishing the work of a new generation of Armenian authors. That's how they met. Their son Rouben was born 14 months ago. When I asked if they were going to stay in Canada, Lorne answered that they weren't certain. There was still lots to accomplish in Armenia. He was happy for Jake's success and for the imminent launch of my novel. I didn't want to ruin his enthusiasm with news of West Beach.

After supper, Lucine put Rouben to bed and had so many questions to ask Abby about life in Canada and whether she thought they could begin a life in Toronto. I had a quiet conversation with Lorne. I told him that whatever success we have had here has been undercut by Detective Jon's ongoing investigation into Al Pommeroy's murder. "What's with that guy? He's relentless," he said. "Maybe we should tell him what happened to get him off our backs."

"I don't think that's a good idea, Lorne," I told him. "In this case, the truth may not be the best way to get clear."

"Why not? We're not responsible."

"Remember that he married Jake's former wife Hannah. There's a lot of tension among the three of them over Jake's return. Jake blames them both for betraying him. I believe that Jon is looking to put us away. That would make his life easier and cleaner. He could say that he saved Hannah from Jake the criminal, and that they could get on with their lives. Then there is the Gladys Crummley affair."

"Jake wasn't responsible for that, was he?"

When I couldn't give Lorne a straight answer, he looked away. "We're screwed, Jacob. How the hell did we get wrapped up in this?" He went silent for a moment then said, "Maybe we should invite him to Port Hope and give him a demonstration of how it happened." He looked at me and smiled. "Just kidding. Just…."

"Not so funny, Lorne. No one must know. Not even your wife."

"Don't worry. I've had no reason to tell her."

We finished our wine and set them up in the spare room. I told them that Jake will be coming over for breakfast tomorrow. "Maybe, after that, the three of us can go over to Waterman's to compare notes and see if the espresso is still good."

"Yes, that's a good idea," Abby said. "I'll take Lucine and Rouben out for a walk along Bloor Street. Don't worry about us, we'll have lunch somewhere expensive." And with that we all went to bed. Lorne and I may have tried to work out the plots of our new stories as we tossed and turned during the night, but all we thought about was the vexatious detective who was ruining our sleep and was inadvertently impelling our stories into a mystery that ended with the disappearance of a certain detective from 53 Division and three writers looking for absolution.

28

Another lousy night with little sleep. After two hours of staring at the ceiling, I got out of bed quietly and went to the kitchen. There was Lorne leaning over the counter, pouring himself a cup of coffee. "You, too," he said with a knowing smile. "I figured as much. Shall I pour one for you?" "It's this thing," he said as he handed me the cup. "We didn't go out of our way to harm anyone. The guy surprised us. It was a premeditated attack on Jake."

"You're right," I told him. "I just opened the door to find out what he wanted. Maybe he lunged at the door when I opened it, and that knocked him off balance. To tell the truth, I don't remember anymore."

"Neither do I. It happened so quickly. I was sitting in the front seat, but it is clear in my mind that he wanted to do Jake harm."

"It was an unfortunate accident." We went silent for a while and drank our coffee. "The problem is," I said, "We didn't call for help. The second strike against us is that we took him to Port Hope."

"Why the hell did we?" The words constricted in Lorne's throat.

"And the third, we dumped him in the lake."

"Detective Jon told me Al was dead before being put in the lake."

"You saw how Jake jumped on him and pushed his face under water. Man, he has issues; now we're all involved. Why do you think I went to Armenia? I wanted start over clean and write my stories."

"Yeah, and now you're back, and Detective Jon is still sniffing around, and we're all feeling guilty. But tell me this, Lorne, would we be feeling the same way now if Jon and the police had classified it as an unsolved murder and weren't even aware of us?"

We sat on the couch in front of the television and pondered this as we stared at the dark screen blankly, trying to come up with an idea, a harbour we could sail into for shelter and safety. But this storm wasn't going to blow over.

In the morning after breakfast, we all walked down to Bloor Street then after hugs and kisses, we left Abby, Lucine and Rouben and went down St. George Street to Harbord and the café. As we approached the front door, I was surprised to feel that so much time seemed to have passed and that so many things had changed, but when we entered, I found that it was yet another illusion of time and a guilty mind. When we entered, Harold, came out from behind the counter and shook our hands. "Welcome back, Lorne. Great news about Jake, eh? And congratulations to you, Jacob. I hope you're going to find space on the back cover to mention that your work was created here thanks in no small part to my espresso." Harold looked around and asked us to follow him into the back. "I think you should know that the detective has been hangin' round, askin' questions of the regulars about the three of you. Yeah, he was here just last Wednesday. No one told him a thing other than that you're writers and sit together to talk and drink coffee. If he comes back, I'll let you know."

"Damn it," Lorne spat out the words under his breath, "is nowhere safe from this guy?" After hearing what Harold had told us, we didn't feel like hanging around. We thanked Harold and headed out, keeping a lookout for Jon.

As we walked north up Huron Street past the Robarts Library, I asked Lorne why he stayed in Armenia. "I mean I can understand your wanting to get away, but why did you stay?"

"It's not so difficult to understand, Jacob. I can relate to the people and the situation in the country. They had been suppressed for so long and exchanged the communists for the oligarchs. The young people are dynamic; they're searching for avenues to explore their creativity in ways that express both their individualism and their attachment to their new society. Remember that Armenia is a very old country. The Turkish genocide in 1915 practically destroyed everything that held the country together. Turkey denies that a genocide took place. Up to 1,500,000 Armenians were killed. Today, corruption is rampant, but the country is forward looking, while respecting its past. It's quite exciting to live there. It reminds me a little of Israel. Then there are the ongoing hostilities with the Azeris over Karabakh, the Armenian enclave, *Artsakh*, as Armenians call it. Every day you feel here are so many tensions, but you work through them. Electricity is more reliable now. Good food is available. Like Jews, Armenians have a long memory. Writing a political thriller in this environment is exciting."

We walked up Avenue Road towards my place. "Jacob, let me add finally that my greatest reasons for staying in Armenia now are Lucine and Rouben. My royalties and translation rights, meagre as they are and the few invitations to speak abroad, allow us the chance to live modestly and occasionally to travel. I think I have found a home." I told him that I was happy for him and that I would miss him. He put his hand on my shoulder and said, "You can always come and visit."

146

After supper, Lorne surprised us when he said that they were leaving for Montreal in the morning to visit Lucine's aunt. We had a quiet moment together before bedtime during which he confided in me that he didn't trust the detective. "He's too zealous for such a case that could be explained away. You heard Jake. Al Pommeroy was a gangster and a killer. He must have had a lot of enemies who wanted him dead; so why is Jon harassing us? He's working on a hunch and he has it in for us, especially Jake."

"You know why. It's about Jake and Hannah."

"Well, we're going to France after we leave Montreal. I won't tell you where in case you're forced to cough up information under a rubber hose treatment or waterboarding." I looked at him in his eyes. "You're wise not to. At my age, I would break easily and quickly."

We took them to the Porter Airline terminal at the waterfront and bade them farewell, not knowing if we would ever see each other again. "Come visit us in Yerevan," Lucine told us. "There are many stories waiting for you there." Lorne and his family flew off. I was saddened by his departure. I wondered if Abby and I should get lost in Israel for a year.

Neither of us felt hungry after we saw our friends off. We napped a little then ate an Israeli salad and a few sardines for supper. After, I dried the dishes and put them away. Abby came over to hug me. She said she was tired and wanted to read in bed before sleeping. I kissed her and told her I wanted to check something in my father's notebooks and that I would join her shortly. I was certain I had seen reference to Armenians in one of his journals dating from 1966. I was anxious to find it.

November 17, 1966

My dear Jacob, I have been filling these notebooks since before the Nazi vermin invaded Salonica and destroyed our community. I managed to save a few and bring them with us on our perilous journey that eventually brought us to New York. At that time, the American government was run by bystanders. We were unable to enter directly as refugees and obliged to go to Brazil first while Jewish agencies worked to bring us to America. Emil Fackenheim wrote that thou shalt not be a bystander. It's still true. Since that time, I have been filling many notebooks regularly in part to restore sanity to an otherwise agitated life but more so to leave you a legacy, some inkling of how our family fared after inquisitions and invasions. What you will find is intended as a focused history as well as a warning.

In another journal dated 1981, there is this entry from December 28.

Our neighbours down the hall, Ara and Elizabeth Hagopian, invited us over for a meal. We often offer each other such invitations. They were rescued after the Armenian Genocide by Near East Relief and brought to Ellis Island then settled in New York. He is a medical doctor. Elizabeth volunteers at their church as there are always new refugees arriving. Late at night after our meal, we often share stories of our survival and our hopes to be able to continue to celebrate and share our heritages. Tonight, before you returned from the library, Ara thought that we, that is our families, suffered the same fate. However, with the passage of time, he said that the Armenian Genocide, though still very painful, has been softened and begun to be integrated into the general stream of history and enriched and challenged by debates around World War I. They rob the dead of their particularity, that they were selected for destruction because they were Armenian. The Armenian Genocide exists less and less in lived memory, 65 years after the beginning of the massacres as more and more of the survivors have died. Always so much talk of death. Fortunately, Elizabeth served us her famous Armenian coffee and a plate of *loukoum*. from Turkey.

The very scale of the destruction, Ara continued, and the crime make it very difficult to contemplate. The television series, "Holocaust," in 1978, despite the criticism levelled by Elie Wiesel and others at least raised the consciousness of what had happened. One must comprehend, he said, if one is to remember. The vastness of the evil must not prevent comprehension in order for memory to follow.

Ara told us of an important moment in Armenia in 1965. Armenians gathered spontaneously and marched in large numbers to the Swallow's Nest, the national memorial to the Genocide to commemorate 50 years since the beginning of the deportations and massacres in 1915. The sudden outpouring of anger and desire surprised the soviets who were unable to control it. "You see," he said, "such a memorial is a way of inscribing on the earth what a powerful group did to a weaker and vulnerable group. The memorial's presence is a resistance to the eroding of memory." Ara raised his hand as he spoke, "Here is the difference between our two peoples. We Armenians want the world to remember what happened to us in 1915; our Jewish brothers and sisters don't want the world to forget what happened to them

149

before and during World War II. The Turks deny still today that there was a genocide. Unbelievably, there are those who deny the Holocaust. We need to find listeners.

The Hagopians never had children. Ara told me they didn't want to bring children into such a world. They both cared for you very much, Jacob, as I'm sure you remember. The world needs more Armenians, I told him. But they were past having children and lived their lives being happy and being sad as their survival was not only a blessing for them but also a source of anguish.

29

It's early fall. The leaves of the trees on our street have just begun turning. Soon there will be an explosion of reds and yellows and before long, geese will fly south. The weather will get crisp and cold, and snow will cover everything. It will be a time for cardigans and heavy sweaters, a late morning cup of coffee, sitting on the couch with a new book, or sitting at my desk, working on a new story or rereading my father's notebooks from which I have learned so much. I understand how important they can be to keep track of events and clarify thoughts. Thus, I've begun keeping a journal as my father had done, except mine will begin by a voyage to Salonica; whereas, my father's charts his permanent departure from his home.

Ari Grimm phoned today to say that my book is about to go into full production. They will begin with a run of 500 hardcover copies and another 600 in paperback to test the market. Interviews and readings have already been arranged. I do a quick calculation. In a year, the royalties earned might just get us to Collingwood to spend one night in a resort with a nice meal. Maybe. I've never been in it for the money. Our pensions are enough to keep us comfortable and happy if we don't do anything foolish.

I hear Abby open the door and place her things on the hall table. I'm anxious to see her and put down my pen and go to greet her. We go into the kitchen where she lays down an envelope on the table and hugs me then turns me around in a circle. "You're in a playful mood," I tell her. "You know, Jacob, sometimes you just have to be." I kiss her and ask her if she is hiding anything. "I come home happy and flirtatious, and you immediately think there's something going on. I think you're the strange one."

During supper, she keeps on smiling. Then just as we finish our meal, she slides the envelope she had laid on the table earlier towards me. "This came for you today." I pick it up and look at it. There is no writing on it. Abby clears the plates from the table as if she is uninterested in what I am doing. Even when I open it, she focuses on putting the dishes in the machine. I pull out two plane tickets for Athens then Thessaloniki. "What's that?" she asks coyly; then a beautiful smile brightens her face. "Apparently, my love," I said matter-of-factly, "we're going to Salonica."

"Are you happy, Jacob?" She's worried that I might not be, given all that we have talked about going.

I rise and put my arms around her. "Thank you, my love. I know it's something I have to do. I'm happy we'll be together."

Up in the air over the Atlantic. Nothing but blue sky, puffy white clouds and the dull drone of the engines. After a supper of steamed vegetables in pasta and tomato sauce, Abby leans her head on my shoulder and closes her eyes. There are still hours to go before landing in Athens and taking the connecting flight to Thessaloniki. I try but am unable to sleep. The whole purpose of the trip churns in my stomach. I keep telling myself I'm going back to the source. My father would have believed that. I am not at all sure I do. And when we arrive in Salonica, Thessaloniki, what will I be looking for? My parents' community has all but disappeared. Any remnants of our family and home have been plowed under in order to rebuild the new city of Thessaloniki. What am I looking for? How will any of this be meaningful? I'm too removed from it all. Abby lived in Israel; it's a living part of her. No doubt we will attend a service in one of the three remaining synagogues in the city. Some will want to call it a return, but I come as a nervous tourist. There is no memory here for me to recover even less to understand. I can't construct memory; I have no memory to intrude in my life and be part of my identity.

The day before we departed, I received a letter from Detective Jon wishing us a safe journey. What nerve. It was followed by this: "Some new evidence has been discovered that has a direct bearing on the death of Al Pommeroy. I'll be expecting you, Jake and Lorne to come in for interrogation when you return. I'll send officers to let you know when." That bastard. As the plane climbs higher to avoid dark clouds and an impending storm up ahead, all I can think of is Al Pommeroy cracking his head on the hydrant and Jake holding his head underwater at West Beach.

Then the turbulence begins. We bounce along, drop suddenly into an air pocket and rise on a column of warm air then are buffeted. The plane shakes violently. Some passengers start screaming; others pray. Abby tucks her arm in under mine and pulls herself closer to me. She whispers, "We're going to be okay, aren't we, Jacob?" "Yes, my love," I tell her. "We have my book launch in two months." It's a smart Alec remark that doesn't comfort her. The captain's calm voice over the p. a. system does little to assure everyone. The plane suddenly lurches forward and up; then everything goes quiet and calm. The baby cradled in her mother's arms two seats ahead still cries. People around us cross themselves then spontaneously begin chanting a Greek prayer. All I keep thinking during the ordeal that lasts perhaps fifteen minutes is that this is the result of my choices and that I am what I have made myself. It becomes immediately obvious that the existentialist's creed is of small or no comfort at all when one is bouncing around thirty thousand feet in the air over the Atlantic. Then another gem from the creed comes to mind, "You can always make something out of what you've been made into." A little late for that. I don't think I'll be able to rise above my fate as Camus believed Sisyphus did pushing that bloody stone uphill. I tell myself that I should limit my expectations given my mortality. Now that I've reminded myself once again that there is no ultimate hope, I start laughing. "What's wrong with you, Jacob?" Abby asks, puzzled and annoyed. She needs comfort and me to be present. "Sorry, my love," I tell her. "It's just a moment of clarity." We hug each other tightly and say, "I love you," to each other. The plane settles back on its flight path. People are talking, relieved the ordeal has passed. Alcohol is served. Even the baby has stopped crying. Abby puts her head on my shoulder. I can feel her calm breaths and live in their rhythm. A moment of clarity. It feels as if the world has just given me a kick in the backside. Nothing else matters to me except Abby and our love for each other.

The first thing we decide to do in Salonica is to tour the city and visit the Jewish Museum of Thessaloniki where we learn that the Holocaust Memorial in Freedom Plaza had recently been vandalized with swastikas drawn all over it and that other similar incidents have occurred in other Jewish sites. It's never going to end. I know I'm not going to find here the world my parents fled. There are perhaps one thousand Jews left. I'm uncomfortable, ill at ease here, restless and eager to move on. I tell Abby I want to leave and return home after visiting Athens so I can continue studying my father's journals.

There is more truth and honesty in them; I can hear my mother's and father's voices when I read their words. Here there is only sadness and regret.

The clash between the gleaming new modern city of Thessaloniki that feels a reluctant necessity to honour the Jewish community which formed the majority of the population until the war destroyed everything and the reality of my father's notebooks is almost too much to bear. What makes this worse for me is that all of my father's journals that contained stories and reminiscences of our family and the Jewish population were left behind when they escaped that fateful night. There was no room in his valise for the past contained in all his books. Two notebooks, pen and ink were all he allowed himself as he and my mother headed out on a perilous journey and an uncertain future.

As we sat in a taverna for our last meal in the city before flying back to Athens then a few days later to Toronto, I thought of what my parents witnessed and how the destruction of Jewish presence in Salonica and the loss of so many family members must have weighed on them terribly all their lives. They escaped while others didn't or couldn't and perished in Auschwitz or Treblinka. My father was a true witness. Not only had he observed what the Nazis did to the Jews, himself included, but for the rest of his life once he and my mother settled in New York, he wrote about it and spoke out in his classes, at synagogues and at conferences. His voice was one of authority. "I was there. I saw it. I am telling you." He received many letters of thanks from compatriots who had also survived. Not only did he give voice to those who were silenced, but he also preserved their names as much as he could and compiled lists of names and wrote brief biographical sketches of each with their family connections and printed them off. He was a memorialist, an archivist, and an educator as well as a writer of fiction. His greatest gift as a short story writer, I believe, was that he was able to make fiction so real that you forgot you were reading words on a page. We try to arrange the world in a way that is comforting. Fiction in all its varieties always has a beginning, a middle and an end. The enduring value of the writing my father left was his ability to erase the distinction between what was experienced and what he wrote. When I read through his notebooks, I can feel his voice calling to me. I can't live his life, nor can I let him live mine. But the work must continue. There is a maxim, an ethical teaching by Rabbi Tarfon that I read many years ago in the *Pirkei Avot, Chapters or Ethics of the Fathers*, complied sometime in the second century CE. "It is not your duty to finish the work, but neither are you at liberty to neglect it." This puts the dilemma and the necessity for responsibility in a stark light and is a call to action.

I put my file of notes away and take out a new notebook, fill my fountain pen with a new sapphire ink I had purchased last week and begin plotting a new work dedicated *To My Parents, Shalom and Rose Levy.*

It's several weeks later on a Friday. The temperature has dropped dramatically for late November. Snow falls on the city, leaving a thin white blanket over everything. A courier buzzes from the lobby with a package from Ari Grimm that needs my signature. He has sent the proof of my book with the cover. Ari writes in the note accompanying the book, "Go through it line by line. Make sure it's perfect. Check the cover to make sure we got it right. As soon as I hear from you, we can begin full production." I show Abby. She cradles it as if it were a newborn. "*Mazal tov*, my love. May there be many more." I kiss her tenderly. "Now, leave me," she says. "I still have to prepare for Shabbat." Although we are secular, we still do candle lighting, then drink sacramental wine from a kiddush cup, eat challah followed by a special meal together on Shabbat. We remember family who are no longer with us.

After the meal, Abby and I clean up and wash the dishes. I go to my writing room and look at the proof of my book. When I open it, I can smell the odour of paper and ink that makes the pulse quicken. Shortly after reading the front material, the phone rings.

"Jacob? It's Jake."

"Jake, how are you?"

"Well I was doing okay up until a few minutes ago."

"Why? What happened?"

"The knock at the door, Jacob. The bloody knock at the door."

"What do you mean?"

"Detective Jon sent two policemen to deliver a message. We have to be in his office at 10 am this Monday."

"We?"

"He wants the three of us. Lorne's in Armenia."

"That's the detective's problem."

"They found something. I know it."

"Jake, we shouldn't be discussing this over the phone."

"They're coming for you, too, Jacob."

"They're just trying to intimidate us. Be calm."

I look out the window and see a cruiser parked in the visitor's parking lot. There are boot imprints in the clean snow leading to the main entrance to my building. I sit down in my

chair and hold my book. I turn to look at Abby and wait for
the buzzer and the knock at the door.

LORNE SHIRINIAN has published 24 books of fiction, drama, poetry and scholarly studies. He is Professor Emeritus of English and Comparative Literature at the Royal Military College of Canada. At present, he is working on two writing projects, *Rendering the Timeline*, a new collection of poetry, and *Intimate Spaces*, a work of fiction that deals with the ongoing anguish of living with the Armenian Genocide.